I0761678

ASHLAND

Dan Simon

ASHLAND

Europa Editions
27 Union Square West, Suite 302
New York NY 10003
www.europaeditions.com
info@europaeditions.com

First publication 2026 by Europa Editions

Library of Congress Cataloging in Publication Data is available
ISBN 979-8-88966-167-2

Simon, Dan
Ashland

Cover design by Stewart Cauley of Pollen

Cover photograph by Asha Manuela Simon, all rights reserved

Prepress by Grafica Punto Print – Rome

Printed in Canada

CONTENTS

What we've never had is a song.
—Robert Hass

. . . there is no more hope of my father's homecoming,
I believe no messages any more . . .
—*The Odyssey of Homer*, Richmond Lattimore trans.,
Book I, l. 413-14

Peel away the things that are always changing, you get the things that never change. Peel away the things that never change, you come to the explosions that detonate slowly over the years. One, two, three—too few to form a pattern.

We call them transformations.

ASHLAND

Part One

Carolyn (1992)

If you come to think of it, there are some women who just don't belong pregnant, not even temporarily. And they have their babies just like everybody else. The moms grow up together with the little girls and boys. You can tell at a glance how it isn't meant to be.

That's mama and me. The lost look passing from her to me that says, We've survived this, and we'll survive what comes next, and whatever comes after that. But since we're human, someday something will happen to us that we cannot survive.

I want to capture all of it. Not just us, but all those who aren't where they're supposed to be. In my life, Edith and Gordon, with their sons, Peter—and Warren. I mean, Geoff. Oh Geoff, the doors you opened for me! Rooms I never entered. Mostly not. But thanks to you I at least began to believe they really do exist if ever I find my way to them again. And I mean Marie and me. The fallacies, the impossibles, the disproofs.

I have always understood myself to be a bit like smoke, a mysterious interruption between earth and sky, a nameless silhouette, a shadow, or like when you rip a page out of a book, how it doesn't tear straight but yields and resists, or a flowing body of water, the way it folds back over itself, tugging forward and edging sideways.

Do other girls think of themselves as some natural occurrence, a straight line that issues forth from a grown woman and a grown man, the continuation of familial love? People like me know in our selves we might not love, or have enough love, or enough self, that these are choices, and artifices, and not choices at all, impediments in us as we point and poke this way and that to find the love that might send us forth like a cannonball out of a cannon. We're doubtful that we will ever find it, or even that such a thing truly exists. This too—all of it, nonsensically—is exactly who we are, and we may as well accept our selves instead of trying forever to pull in one direction or the other.

I was my own person from the very start, from my birth I mean, someone with my own private life, an old soul they call it. With my mama Ellie so hesitant, I had to be strong. All anybody could hope for for me—all *I* could hope for—was that I'd be different, that I'd break the age-old family tradition of early ruination. Which I never did. No. Running as far and as fast as I can in the exact opposite direction, towards self-determination, I yet continued in the hallowed family tradition. Not as fast as mama, but almost as fast, and these are different times. All things considered, I judge that I engineered my ruination without too long a delay, early enough for there to be at least the small chance of a fruitful afterlife for me, let's say.

Most people don't notice the many minute differences; they think that all cigarette smoke is the same, but nothing could be further from the truth.

Parliament is whitish and on a windless day spirals upwards over us in very skinny wisps without much torque to them, almost-flat ribbons that rise above this slow-moving, almost motionless land of boulders and roads, trees and souls, swaying just a little ever so slowly from side to side.

To give you an idea of the range: Old Gold smoke is billowy and yellowish and tends to clump up. Camel is more or less like Old Gold, a little less yellow and a little slenderer, but very similar. Marlboro is flecked with black and gray. Marlboro

Lights produce a thinner, more ominous-looking smoke than Marlboro Reds. Pall Mall smoke travels wet and puffy, like tiny storm clouds approaching, and those are my favorites, though I don't smoke them regularly. Luckys make smoke that's white and rich like whipped cream.

And so on.

In the same way that certain arrivals—births—aren't meant to be but happen anyway, some couplings are destined, irrevocably, and cannot end, even though they do. I am not saying fantastical things, only very matter of fact ones. If you think about it, you will understand me perfectly. I mean, not if you think about it, but if you look closely and recognize what's right in front of you—two human souls in need not of some more general comfort but of something so weirdly specific that it only emanates from one other person, a species connection between two individual entities that exists nowhere else. They are never meant to end. But then they do end. I'm speaking as an observer, of Jennie and Andy of course, for the intense beauty, how like tree roots entwined together they were, so stubborn, and I'm speaking also of mama and me.

I have never seen the Atlantic Ocean, though when I close my eyes I sometimes imagine what it must be like to look out where there is no far shore visible, no end, and this thought pacifies me, produces from a long way off a quiet reasonableness.

I smoke a pack of Parliament Lights a day. Little tombstones you light up and fire off like sparklers. I don't think they'll kill me though. Something else will, and when I have the right reason I'll stop smoking them, stop from one breath to the next, just like that, when it's time.

What my life will be isn't exactly a mystery to me. It is a kitchen drawer that's already full of all the things I think I'll do, that now I know I'll probably never do, and the other things I think I'll never do that are coming towards me all in a rush. And as each one gets closer, I can recognize it, to my great surprise, as mine, and then it hits me. I don't mean metaphorically, I don't mean it hits me like a realization. I mean it gores me and leaves you saying it's anybody's guess whether it shatters a bone or only leaves a deep hole that's going to heal in time or will fester and pustule and rot—and kill me outright.

We are lengths of string, nothing more, fixed at one end, frayed at the other, constantly unraveling.

The flowing water pulls and tugs at us.

We never quite come together. We never quite come undone. And then, all of a sudden, we do come undone.

We live such a short time, hardly more than the blink of an eye. It turns out our circles within circles unravel endlessly, eternal only for the unfinishedness, little more than new beginnings with uncertain prospects. Ah, we accept to go all-in for so little.

Sometimes it can happen that our own private ends seem to fit together with someone else's. The frayed parts get knotted up and the blunted ends grow into each other, or seem to, like the pieces of a puzzle.

I've seen bitter things, and I've seen relief that comes completely unexpectedly, too. I've seen girls discover unforeseen tenderness, for example. One I know marries a man who uses her harshly. Everyone who knows her thinks it's a mistake to marry him. Her husband is diagnosed with chronic emphysema. He can't work, but gets disability payments. He's only twenty-eight, his eyes still ever-restless. Breathes with the assistance of his oxygen tank next to his bed or his chair, like it were his most obedient friend, his faithful hound for the hunting forays he takes in his dreams. Greatly diminished, he still smokes, that other friend for him as it is for me. But he is no longer violent towards her, doesn't have the strength or the inclination, has forgotten that man entirely. It happens. Startling good fortune like that. She had not foreseen an end to him hitting her. Was reconciled to her worser fate and now gets this harmless, broken and good man beside her instead. Sometimes the evil that comes to us has no author, and other times good comes that is just as unexpected and unexplainable. She already loved him without having a good reason, this man who becomes through happenstance someone she could not ever have envisioned, a gentle soul.

I'm Carolyn—to give a name to this voice that is haranguing you—born here in Ashland twenty years ago in March of 1972, March being the last month of true winter this far north. Mama is seventeen years old when she finishes making me and I sally forth. My aunt Jennie, mama's younger sister, is pregnant at the same time as mama. Marie, her eldest, comes in June, three months after me, thank God, when Jennie is only fourteen. This is our auspicious beginning, no one alone for very long. Or to put it a different way, since I have thought about this: The loneliness of an adolescent girl like mama can be the highest mountain crushing down on you, and you make a baby to have some hope of companionship, to produce a daughter who will at least *see* you.

In the year leading up to me, I picture mama very womanly already and at the same time a tomboy and, honestly, a child still, with a lot of ideas in her head about what she might do if ever she does finally grow up and become a woman, very quiet like she still is and very stubborn like she still is. And I want to think my arrival is a blessing on her. But what are you going to do with a baby at seventeen? Nobody can help you until you survive the worst on your own. Not even Jennie can help her, or she Jennie. To get through it, the only way, you separate yourself, transport yourself, not yet realizing the cost, which is to be alone in some sense forever after.

People can see into the future sometimes. And, like it's another future, into the past sometimes too. Marie knows this, and I know it. And sometimes being able to see far ahead or far behind you means being afflicted with a poet's blindness as to what's right before your very eyes.

I'm a writer. It's the only thing I know for sure, and I don't know how. It's something that no one gave me or said, which is partly how I know it, it's something that comes entirely from inside. From time to time other people do recognize this thing in me, whether you want to call it an ability, a calling, or whathaveyou.

Some of the things that happened before Marie and I were born I can see so clearly I can reach right out and touch them.

Other things I know happened I wouldn't believe even if I'd been there to watch them unfold and had pictures to prove it.

I want to tell you: the town of Ashland has its own lost look, as if it were a matter of its own survival to ignore, to tamp down, to pave over, to batter. To domesticate roughly, when all around you, out there, the wildness of rock, of woods, of ice and rushing water taunts your domestications. So only here, in the little town, can you even try it.

The Squam Lake Woolen Mill is established in 1840. The words are carved in the lintel stone on one of the buildings over there. They rename it the L.W. Packard Company when a new owner buys it at the beginning of the century. Some members of the family, the Gliddens, still live here, including Shirley Splaine who creates the Doll Museum and a few others. Most of the red brick buildings along the river below the drop aren't in operation now, just a bare bones activity there. The storefronts along Main Street, same story. There was a grand hotel and all the rest. Back in the 1800s, tourists came from Boston on the train and disembarked in Ashland, then went by riverboat or horse drawn carriage over to the even grander hotel resorts in Holderness or on Squam Lake. Now Paquette's Hardware still does all right, and Bob's Shurfine, the grocery store. But you get the feeling that it's a ghost town compared to what was here once.

Mama and Jennie lived with my two great-aunts in the house on River Street, overlooking Squam River just before it sluices into town. Before the drop the river's all bravado. Then it's hammered and stowed away and spit out by the mills. A pristine and vibrant masterpiece when it enters our town, depleted and nearly lifeless at the other end.

But I don't think it was always like this. We're here to witness the last days of the mill town existence. From more work than there were men and women to do it, to not much work at all. Thankfully, there's always the Pemigewasset, our northern Mississipi if you will. The Pemi accepts the remnants of the Squam after it grinds through town, rescuscitating it. Birds come and crawfish and eagles, pickerel and bass, peregrine falcon, great blue heron, and all the rest.

A hundred years ago the Squam was still a logging river. I've seen pictures of it clogged with the trunks of seventy foot long trees—masts they called them—and men like titans rolling them in a dance on the water, and here and there barges and steamboats with wood-burning furnaces and tall smokestacks, and the men smiling wide with a fullness and a grimness and a gladness that hasn't sat on any man's face here since then, I'd say.

We never consider the river's fate. Maybe because the wrenching apart of the river is so like the wrenching apart of ourselves.

But once every person here must have felt its wildness in them, teaching them, our highway long before I-93, our university before there was Plymouth State.

The house on River Street keeps the lives of the women living in it separate and apart, as places do where there isn't a lot of talking: two old women and two young mothers, still girls themselves. Each person so alone there.

I think about how Jennie and mama favor certain small signs between them, gestures that are familiar to me for the unfinishedness of them, because they learn them as children from their own mother, my granma, who doesn't stay around long enough for them to get her tics exactly right. Jennie's far-away look. And how mama taps my hand with her fingers.

I can close my eyes and reach all the way back to her—my granma—like she were a girlfriend and not have that be a fruitless exercise. I know her. I am her. She was once a girl just like I am. She has to leave her world behind in the same way that I must—even if for her it is to escape the approaching war and for me I don't know what's coming, only that I have to leave too, leave all this, leave what I love.

She looks around her and weighs her assets which are her thick auburn hair, her wide hips and buttocks, her shapely feet, her slender shoulders and neck, her laughing eyes, the same as mama's and mine. Not a bad portfolio, enough to weigh in the balance against the war that's coming. And she too is both a woman and a child when necessity drives her to leave her home. It takes her three months to deliver herself to a port city in the next country over and then to traverse the greatest of oceans, the one that is so near that I have never seen, in steerage like wave after wave of European immigrants before her. She makes landfall in the port of New York and before long meets a boy who speaks her language and they both know their chances together are better than their chances alone. I know all this. In a tingling way. That is, I can feel her as she herself feels, inhabit her skin and her possibilities just as she does. I see her in Ellie, and I see her in the mirror and I see her when I try as I often do to look inside myself. And each time, or let's say, oftentimes, mama and I both seem to be mostly her and only a little ourselves and so, yes, my unfathomable granma, I know her.

She comes to Ashland with her girls, without a husband or companion now. She has parted from the boy she made them with. I don't know why, pulled apart after three years because whatever it is keeping them together isn't strong enough against the pull of the currents taking her. Or because she hasn't come all this way to put herself into the hands of a man from home. Or is it because having her girls, my Ellie and Jennie, just takes her from him as it can sometimes do? So she cuts loose from him and comes here to Ashland where she has two aunts who live in a big house by a river, like in Europe, to live with her daughters, without him.

And already in her the possibility that she might choose to leave mama and Jennie with the aunts and move on, to save herself. I feel her restlessness. Her rules aren't anybody else's. I know she keeps moving, exploring the region on her own, looking for something, I don't know what. By the time mama is five and Jennie is two, starting around 1961, when not just her but the whole country is beginning to stir, she's already away more than she is here. Her girls are growing up. But she has already been gone for months, maybe years.

I don't know whether she dies or finds her way. I can only say that there is a quietness that's come down to me that lets me feel as if I do know. Not the particulars of what happens to her ten or twelve years before I come into this world, but something else, some quality in her. Confident that her girls are being looked after, she decides to be someone other than the woman she's supposed to be. And she doesn't die, I feel I know she doesn't. She escapes, her freedom coming—as I suspect real freedom always does—at the greatest possible price. You pay for your freedom the most you possibly can, that's the rule, and not a penny less. This most precious thing, you say to the seller, I want it badly, I must have it. But I must bargain for it, so tell me, what is the very most I can pay? Let the price be the very highest, I want to pay the most, not a penny less.

And when she finally dies, she will die a free woman who has led her life as she wanted, with decency to the end because nothing she does is done frivolously, even abandoning her daughters is done according to some higher law, unspeakable and inevitable. She dies an admirable woman, and still a beauty, because what she does she does guided by an inner compass and this is clear to anyone with eyes to see even if there are no words to explain or decipher the meaning. Her head held high, aged now, in some town where she is loved, somewhere north of us, in Canada, or over in Vermont, where there are ten thousand trees for every person and the towns are little miracles, doll towns set against the vastness of forests.

In the photographs I have of her when she is young, this granma of mine looks very old-world—big in the hips and cheekbones and with a strong laughing face, not a tragic-looking face at all. She makes me proud.

Mama never says a bad word about the boy who got her pregnant with me. Her pride prevents her. And anyway, there is no future for them. It is a simple truth. They aren't even grown up yet. So I know that if—before I'm born—my father came around with flowers and a ring, she would have shut the door on him, closed it quietly but firmly. And anyway, he never did.

He's just a boy, a little younger than her, but not by much and even less mature of course. I guess she sees him around town sometimes after I'm born, and hardly says a word. If there's one thing that's clear to us, it's that them getting married would be the worst of all possible outcomes, a murder of souls—hers, his, mine. A serial killing.

~

When I'm four, my father's mother comes to see us. Her place is too big for her to live in by herself, she says. She wants us to have it. She doesn't want any money.

Mama listens, standing just inside the door of the River Street house, while this other grandmother I don't know stands outside, below her, on the top step. I can see mama doesn't want to thank her. She knows we're due something from her son and her. Mama owns her hurt and it's precious to her. So she just holds on to it for the longest minute.

But then she steps down, slightly swaying, almost swooning, and lets the older woman hold her. And when mama speaks, pulling herself gently away again but with her arms held out and her hands still on the other woman's shoulders, my mama's voice is delicate and strained as she says we'll take care of the house, and that this woman we hardly know must come and visit us whenever she likes so we can get to know her better. And then she takes the other woman in her arms again, commiserating with her, and for just a second there are both their shoulders lightly trembling. This moment and how hard it is for mama I remember like it just happened. After four years, what my grandmother is doing is the right thing finally, the first right action after a period of empty silence from that side of the family. So they're both taken aback by it, both the giver and the receiver, and there's this closeness between them that neither one of them can deny, however much mama might want to. The closeness moves both these women all the more because it's kind of impersonal and comes without all the usual niceties of conversation in Ashland between grown-up women, a certain falseness that takes the pressure off and is at heart a kind of unspoken surrendering to stronger forces. This encounter, by contrast, is without any falseness whatsoever. We can already feel how our new circumstance is going to change everything for us. And then mama turns around and I think that this is the first time she lets me see on her face what I have cost her, and doesn't hide from me just how bad things have been for us up to now.

We leave the River Street house. Where we're going is only three and a half miles from Ashland, but we will come to know it as *our place*. Mama and I take our own private road through the woods, and we have the big brown house in the middle of the fields, at our end of Willow Lake, all for ourselves.

At first we half expect our new old house will be taken from us at any moment. That's how good it is to have it! It's all too new to us to be permanent. We fear a firestorm, a flood, or lightning fires—and because of how high on the hill it sits, lightning does strike on a regular basis, severing the upper branches of the tallest white pine, the soldiers that ring the house at the top of the road, several of them now mutilated from lightning, though still alive somehow. Our sudden good fortune takes getting used to—like we're survivors of something here, and at the same time intruders. We belong, but only by chance.

The young man—the boy—that my father still is only left Ashland for good earlier this spring, his departure being the trigger that prompts his mother to reach out to us. In her sudden loneliness, I imagine. How being abandoned schools her, a harsh result that finds kindness in her since nothing would have prevented her from coming to us much sooner had she wanted to, but she would never have done it earlier. She would have feared a chain reaction. My father's mother says it's for the best. She says having her son on his way and us settled in the big brown house is a great load off her mind. I don't know. She lives in a half-truth world, and with the weight full on her of all the unspeakable parts. She says things always turn out for the best. I feel for her, since it's not true of course. Maybe what she really means is, Things *never* turn out for the best. She's found a second floor apartment for herself over the Five and Dollar in town—and changed places with us, become almost homeless so we can have our home. Mama is twenty-one now. My father is still nineteen.

Mama sings to me sometimes when we walk along together, exploring the property, the minutes and sometimes the hours stretching on and on, sing-songing in her own particular way. And to me the sounds are of a piece now with other melodious sounds here—the grasses in the wind, and the rustling and creaking sounds of everything growing, or a branch falling thunderously or a big animal crashing in with no regard for the noise it makes. Bear and moose can be loud, but then deer mostly make no noise at all, so it's always a surprise when we see them appear, better than anything.

Jennie and Marie come to visit, bearing the latest news from River Street. Things are slowly changing on River Street too, Jennie says. Yes, really they are—her words uncomfortably close and far-away.

My one great-aunt carries a cane on each arm, and the other one wears long skirts, and they both have heavy bracelets and necklaces, like in the old country, and when they come down the stairs together it is like an infernal machine descending. Those are Jennie's words, spoken in wonderment. The River Street House isn't winterized, and ours isn't either, not really. So when the real cold and the winter storms come we're in our mamas' beds to keep warm, Ellie and me out here, the furnace in the basement roaring and making the whole house tremble and shake, Jennie and Marie in town with the great-aunts where the neighbors' dogs start howling and then the ladies sing along, making some noise the best defense against storms in town. And the most curious part is that there being no men around does leave something missing in both our houses. You feel that in a storm.

The worst stories that Jennie regales us with are the old ones, and mama and I love them the most. I don't know why, but maybe it's because, no matter how terrible things got, we came through it. The worse it is in the living, the more we laugh in the telling. There's a wide streak of meanness in the great-aunts towards the younger women who still have their whole lives ahead of them. Kids in town have it in for Jennie and Ellie, kids their same age they were with at school before our moms had Marie and me. But more often it's the great-aunts and their meanness. Jennie and mama haven't done anything to anybody, but having us is like doing something horrible to the whole town; it isn't just our business, it's everybody's. When mama and Jennie first take us out in our strollers they put stones in their pockets to throw back in case there's trouble. Neither mama nor Jennie ever say that the year of our births and the next year and the year after that is more trouble than dying in childbirth would have been, but that idea is in the air—a tragedy and loss of life is something people here know how to handle gracefully, but lives that aren't lost, that are found instead, well that's a different story.

Were all the stories true? Oh, there's no saying what is or if anything is, or what isn't. For us, for Marie and me, it's never so much a question of what's true or not true. What matters is what's said, what breaks the looming silence of unspoken things, the small islands of sounds set against the vastness of all that's unnamed. And no matter what it is that can be said aloud we always understand to be a kind of rescue. Oh my words, my words.

Carolyn (1988)

The town of Ashland rises between two rivers, but you'd never know it. Driving northeast from here to Holderness you sidle along Squam River, then Little Squam lake, and there's that feeling of being beside water. Going the other way, northwest towards Plymouth, you cross a high steel bridge over the inexhaustible Pemigewasset just outside of town, and again there's the nearness of the river and the feeling of a moving body of water that is traveling with you. South of town, Rte. 3 finds the Pemigewasset again and there are some campgrounds with river rafting and tubing. But here, on Main Street and all around the town, it is a darkly kept secret that we're bounded by water on three sides.

Outside of town what you see mostly are farmhouses and New England homesteads. In town there are rooming houses and cottages for one or two families, built for millworkers. Up on Highland Street are some fine mansions. Along Main Street, the ground floor windows are low and tall in the old brick edifices, and there are wide granite steps where I like to sit sometimes. There's just something halfway about the town. Halfway victories, halfway defeats, not necesssarily sad but for the halfwayness itself. People always telling you how important school is, but it doesn't prepare us for the things we'll actually go and do when we're done. We're mostly wasting our time here. And then you graduate.

I am sixteen and a sophomore when I sign up for my first

writing workshop at Plymouth State, technically as an auditor so I don't have to pay. It meets twice a week right after school lets out. I take the bus from Ashland and then run the last part of the way, not to be late. The other students are older, but that doesn't mean anything to me. I remember my first impression of Geoff standing at the blackboard spelling his name. It is as if every other strange thing I've ever seen moves aside to make room for the strangeness of him.

After a little while he walks over to the door, closes it and starts talking to us on his way back to his desk. Geoff's body is weird. Something about how he moves. He's tall, and his body is loose, almost too loose. I stare at him on the first day, trying to understand, thinking for some reason that his body language is saying the same things he is saying with words in his introductory speech, which I am already struggling with. He moves like a friendly monster. Peaceful and at the same time ruthless, his soft voice and the gentle cast of his eyes, together with the feeling that he doesn't suffer fools.

It turns out he's an avid reader of our work. At the end of each week we give him our pages, and when he arrives for the next class it's with a fire in his eyes, his hands clasping the bundle of pages to his chest. My classmates are an odd group: people who want to write, but who know they're probably not going to go far, because they don't have any of the advantages.

Geoff takes me to be *sui generis*, he says, by which I understand him to mean I'm a local creation, like New Hampshire maple syrup, and in my writing I don't seem to be imitating anyone in particular. He tells me the second week of class that he hasn't seen one like me before and doesn't think he ever will again. He looks happy when he says that. He thinks I have talent coming out of my ears. And how rare genuinely gifted people are. He says most people would never want to be writers if they had any idea what it takes. He also says most of those that really are gifted have fantasies of being just like everyone else.

His actual words are, That's what we mean by success. It means talented people being rewarded so that they can have the things that everyone wants and in that way become normal.

I'm sixteen. I don't really think he should be saying any of these things to me. But I like him because he is just saying what comes into his head, not censoring himself. I don't think he's trying to be nice just for the sake of being nice. I've never met someone before who thinks I'm talented.

I grow up reading books. I'm always stopping by the Ashland Town Library after school. I know people will say they were changed by one particular book they read. But for me it isn't like that. I read everything I can get my hands on. There's no one book. Mostly, I'm not even reading good books, never mind great ones. No one tells me anything. I read romances and laugh out loud. I mean they're just so funny! I like reading mysteries. Ellery Queen! But almost nothing I read feels very real to me. Mostly, I'm just seeing how other people tell stories, keep you interested, say more than they should and more than they have to. To me, well, writing just means *saving stuff*, socking it away, like having a bank account of precious observations and memories. It means unpacking silences (that most of all), and seeing what silences are made of. It means teasing the individual threads apart—deconstructing, wrecking, destroying.

If you think of music as the spaces between the notes, that's what writing means to me. I read so many books of all kinds that hardly seem written to me.

Look at the mountains, just look at them. That's how long it takes to do anything that will last. It isn't any different for us. We need many, many lifetimes. But we only get one. To me, my afternoons reading, with my father's mother in town sometimes, beside mama a lot, with Edith, the afternoons reading with these women I trust completely, is as close as I could ever get to the other side of the problem of living, and that's writing. You watch the stories unfold. Reading is something we do, a spiritual exercise. With Geoff, I'm having this experience with a man for the first time. My brain resists this and my heart resists this. I am synchronized in my refusal of the idea of a man being able to do this with the necessary tenderness. You have to imagine something first in order to experience it, even when you smash right up against it. A man's tenderness does exist in the same way as talking animals do. You can see it in their eyes. I do believe in the existence of tenderhearted men, I believe they're everywhere, all around us, and animals that can speak intelligently to us of what they see and what their experience is. You just have to be able to understand the ways they communicate these things to us.

CAROLYN (1991)

Our beach and the dirt road to it were bulldozed right over the marsh a decade or more before we got here. And right after mama and I move in, one of the first things mama does is call one of her boyfriends to ask him to bring in another truckload of sand to restore the beach, which hasn't been looked after by my father's mother and her son. And when the friend comes, waving his cap from the cab of the truck, mama and I follow close behind down to the beach carrying rakes, and stand there to watch the beautiful creamy white sand spill out into the water, like fresh paint, and then with our rakes we spread the sand over the grass and weeds and into the water, and neither of us says a word.

The sand here is never alive the way dirt is. You can't shape it or plant in it the way you do with dirt. It lets everything in, holds on to nothing. Any shape it takes is gone with the next rain. The grass and shrubs that grow here are the patchy and ugly weeds that will grow anywhere. Our beach is like an itchy scar, or like when someone says the wrong thing and you know right away that the words can't be taken back, that even after years what was done can't be undone or made right again.

And at the same time our beach is the nicest and most peaceful spot on the entire lake, unnatural and ruined as it is.

And so we accept that the ruined place can also be the welcoming place, where you daydream and wear the sky over you like an old smashed hat, where the sun warms you from above and below, and where you don't have to think about anything.

This is where I learn that the wrong thing can also be just the thing. Long before I could ever have found the words, our beach makes me happy, more so because it's mama's and mine, more so again because it's man-made, and even more so because it's partly man-made by us. Lake and sky, our near mountains, not infinitudes but sweeping proximities that have something of the comfort that comes with just a taste, a promise, of infinitude. It is where our dead might return to us, alive as they ever were, a comfort to us and comforted by us in equal measure.

The funny part is that it's as if everyone knows all about our beach. Since it's the first one off West Shore Road, there are always people coming over asking us if this is the public landing, or just coming in and using it without asking—as if they sense it doesn't belong to anybody.

And if it's me they're asking, I ask them why they want to know. And then maybe I let them come and launch their boats from off to one side, or swim all in a clump, away from us. Until mama makes me stop, saying if we continue that way there'll be no end to the yesses and the next thing you know our beach won't be ours anymore, which scares me into listening to her.

After that I stand my ground and direct folks to the public landing, which is all the way at the other end of the lake on the main road. *Back to the main road and then as far as you can get from where you are now and still have Willow Lake beside you*, I say. And mama is a little to the side facing away but listening, smiling, standing just a little differently than she might have otherwise, for the love of my words, since she wouldn't dare talk that way to anyone, not with such boldness, not even to me.

Our stream used to be called Lent Brook, named after the family that owned this land long before my father's mother did. No one on the lake knows that name anymore, and people talking to me sometimes call it Your brook. But more often they stumble over the problem of naming—the brook over by your place . . . that runs across your property . . . that your road passes over . . . A body of flowing water is free, a visitor rather than a servant of the places it passes through, so I let that be a lesson to me and I don't mind that words elude other people, too. In wet years, the turns become extreme, the brook folding back on itself. And in dry years it straightens out along a shorter, more direct route. In the thaw every spring, usually in April, it turns fierce, what Edith calls *torrid*, when there is a churning upward and the surface is braided with muscle, water pouring down from the surrounding mountains, ice melt—or as Edith put it to me once, Like the backs of Michaelangelo's Slaves. Underneath the lake there are many unseen springs that spew forth the water the mountains are releasing, and it flows silently into the lake from below with an unseen power.

After I graduate, I find work in Plymouth. I get my driver's license, and mama, after much discussion and resistence, lets me drive her car to work and continue to live with her at home. When I'm 19, I get my own car. A girl has to have her own car! I live and work in Plymouth now, where Plymouth State College has landed like a spaceship on top of a village at the southern edge of the northern wilderness. I have two part-time jobs, one at the college and the other at the health food store. The writing classes with Geoff are free for me now as a staffer. I eat all-organic, mostly for free too, since I can take home day-old bread and vegetables past their prime, perishable but not yet perished.

I look after my mom as best I can, making the drive home from Plymouth to Ashland to see her in seventeen minutes flat. Once or twice during the week, always on Sundays. When I drive I don't watch the road. Instead I raise my eyes until I'm looking up at the sky and the clouds, putting my full attention there, driving with my lower peripheral vision, pulling myself along the drifting country road with its wavering orange line down the middle and its frost heaves and looping turns, precisely uncertain and *ravaged*, as you could say I am, pulled along, more passenger than driver.

I am eighteen, nineteen. I always go home to mama on Sundays, when the college and the health food store are closed. Time stops and returns us to our forever years then, and it's never easy for me to leave to come back to Plymouth after seeing mama on Sundays.

My *ambition* in life? I want to drive slower, and slower, and slower. By the time I'm mama's age, thirty-six, I want to drive half this fast. And by the time I'm fifty, if ever I live that long, to go half as fast again. Let all the other cars fall in line behind me and honk to their hearts' content.

On afternoons before mama had a date, we used to sit together while she did her hair and eyes. It's our special time because she is going to be free of me and our life for a few hours and that brings a kind of peacefulness over us. Then I walk myself over to Gordon and Edith's. They're sitting quietly in their screened porch with cocktails in their hands when I arrive, looking out onto the barely stirring surface of the lake as if listening attentively while it explains something to them. Gordon gets up to fix me a juice and a cracker with cheese or sliced fruit, and I take my seat near them. After awhile, we go to the small round dining table set for three. They bring their cocktails and hardly eat, and I share their dinner inattentively too, impatient for the time, afterwards, while Gordon washes up, when I'll nestle on the floor beside Edith's chair, my head on her knee, and she'll read to me in her nasal voice from her only kid's book, the one called *Stories from the Bible*.

The best thing about Edith reading to me is how it isn't her favorite thing to do, especially right after eating. She already did all she would ever have to do in the childrearing department. Her two sons are big grown men now, one a newspaperman in New Zealand, the other a straw-bale builder in Arizona. I'm a different person now, she says. So she always begins mechanically, distractedly, as if forgetting that these are stories that mean something to her. I wait, anticipating the change in her to come. Each time it is as if she were returning from some far-away place, climbing back slowly, arduously, blindly, over obstacles, uphill. So that when she finally begins to let herself be moved by these characters as she reads to me, these suffering women and slaves, these sons and fathers, whose names she loves but has all but forgotten, it is by total enchantment, taking her completely by surprise each time, and then her voice finds the long cadences as the stories become real to her again as if she were telling them to me now for the first time.

Here I am, God, Job cries out when God calls. *Here I am.* Job, Sarah, Naomi, Abraham, Jonah, Rebecca, Rachel, Ruth, Leah. That moment when people in the Bible call out to God for no particular reason other than just to say they are here—another way of saying they believe, since that is surely the meaning—*I am here* for you to call on me, *I am here*, your servant . . . I find all the hope in the world in it, since there is always this embodiment, this sense that just being here where you are, ready for whatever is going to happen next, is enough, is so much. Is almost reckless in fact, nearly hopelessly optimistic.

Edith explains to me once that back then it's not a question of a God with churches in all denominations like now, not a God with followers coming to worship him on Sunday mornings, but instead an illegal and hunted rebel leader of a God after all.

And when Edith is done, sometimes she turns to me with one of her rare smiles and says, A good story is one worth believing in. Already having forgotten that she herself doesn't believe until almost the very last moment right before she closes the book.

Part Two

Gordon (1980)

I'm born in November, 1907, you see. Nineteen-oh-seven. Imagine that!

I come up in the Great Depression as it's now known. My generation, we see just how bad things can get, how downtrodden people can get in heart and mind, and this makes me and those around me adherents of something you might call earned optimism, hard earned and grounded in reality. There's no optimism like that, it has little to do with the flimsy kind.

The most important thing that ever happens to me is meeting Edith. No question. I don't think she would say the same. When I raise my eyes as high as I can, they reach to her. In her case, she's able to cast her sight to further horizons. I take no offense. No, it's something she does for both of us.

We're nature lovers, always have been. There's glory in nature. We have eyes to see that. But there's also something else, which is our discouragement in our fellow humans, and I suppose this fuels our exaltation. We look away from our disappointment in humankind and let nature fill our souls. There is an implied comparison. I won't deny it, though I don't think I've ever said this before to anyone. We aren't quite a part of the things we see, the flora and the fauna and the coursing waters. And the same is true when we are with other people, whether it's in church or when people visit us in our home. We're apart, Edith and me, from any human group or any natural setting, but not in an unkindly way and not in any way you would notice at first.

~

In my childhood, the streets aren't paved. The Ford Model T has only been in production for five years when I'm born. There are cobblestone streets, and cobblestone quaries and men that know how to lay them so they stay in place, and then there are dirt roads that turn to mud in the rain. If you're a boy like me, six or seven years old, sitting on your front steps like I do, when someone comes by in a moving vehicle—it might be the milk truck pulled by a mare, or a man on a bicycle delivering the mail, or, less often, an automobile and driver—you nod and smile and say hello and the man delivering the milk or the mail does too. It's hard not to! I mean, speeding by, well that's a different story. Whizzing by isn't possible in the days when I'm coming up. Of course, by the time I'm a fully grown boy, ten or fifteen years old, that's already changed, all of it.

I remember when men wear boaters, which bespeaks a certain ease in life, aspirationally in most cases. The stock market is churning money and a young man can make some of it without having to work in a factory or on a farm, which leads to a new way of thinking. And the beginning of summer is marked by Straw Hat Day. It really is! The feeling of a great stirring up is in the air. Electric street lamps exist already, but most people haven't seen them yet. There are still gas lamps in the cities, and gas lamp lighter is still a profession that means something. There aren't many tall buildings yet, so you see a lot more of the sun, everyone does. Where we live, the streets at night are dark and good people are home, and go to sleep soon after dark. Refrigeration isn't widespread. Radios aren't either. It all changes soon enough. Radios are all the rage in the '20s. But life goes on, maybe not so differently in most ways from how it does now—which tells you, all these gadgets and things may not be quite so essential as we're told they are. Technology, I mean, and the fast speed of things.

But I have to confess, I have come almost to the opposite conclusion. You think people don't change much, and I've lived long enough to say that even with all the changes I've seen, that's still true. But, at the same time, well, when was it ever possible to gain something without giving something up? I mean, if we want to figure out a new way to live, with gadgets, it has to come at a cost in the things we cherish inside ourselves. Instead of thinking how much we can get and how little we'll have to lose, we ought to start by listing some of the things we're willing to go without.

We don't have movies yet, at least not in New Jersey where we are—in the countryside—though it's suburbs and towns now. And radios aren't transistors yet, but big beehives that take up their place in living rooms, not kitchens, centerpieces of something new in our lives, which is leisure time, as televisions will be later on. The radio has become important though, and being the announcer of a radio broadcast, that's something, you're famous then, almost as famous as the president. And cars are still novelties, not the workhorses they are today. Trains, now trains, that's a different story, because they move along rails, about the same as today, and railway lines have been built across the whole country, from city to city and coast to coast, so trains are the big thing, even more than planes. Open up the world for us, trains and ocean liners. And Pullmen aren't fancy or rich but union men and respected. Many professions wear a uniform that carries with it the dignity and glory of daily work—the coal man, the milkman, the policeman, the fireman, the doctor, all men of course. Women's work in the home takes more hours than the day holds, running a home is a full-time job. Women always have less free time than men do. We glory in a world that lets a person live longer. But as you know, the war shortens the productive lives of millions of men, and changes women's lives forever because the war sends millions of women to do paid work in factories and there's dignity in that.

There are rich and poor, but the thing is there are not very many rich people. They are so few they almost don't matter. Most people are what today you would call middle-class, or lower-middle-class, working people and their families, so the differences between rich and poor are there I suppose, but not in terms of the worth of a person.

A town might have one or two, at most five, rich families. But against the hundreds of families of more modest means, what can that matter? They aren't a class of people, they're outliers, consumers of services and things that have to be made one by one, at a time in our history when we've just learned that you can mass produce things like chairs to provide them to American families at a very reasonable cost, just as we'll learn how to mass produce automobiles and washing machines. Mass production drives the prices down, it means people of modest means can afford to own them. When I'm coming up, I swear to God, the servants of the rich matter much more to the life of the community than the rich do. There aren't enough rich people to support vacation destinations on their own, so vacations have to be priced to suit regular people. Of course the really rich go off to Europe, and sometimes send their children to school in Switzerland and France and England too. And there are enough of them to fill the ocean liners, I suppose. But that's about it. Let them go to Europe and make a spectacle of themselves. There is the feeling in America that they don't matter, that the rich don't matter. The rich aren't part of the general feeling of this place, and it's true too. They just seem preposterous, they aren't considered to be geniuses, or driving the economy, more like scavengers and parasites. There's not much love for them. They only seem to love themselves. I've lived to see all that change in my lifetime, but there's so much honor and pride back then among regular working people and their families, not the sense there is today that having a lot of money is meaningful, is attractive, is beautiful and smart in some very magical way. In my lifetime I've seen art's beauty dim and some of that glow go to money and lucre, but it is like pouring water and sunshine on a slab of rock and expecting it to sprout forth!

I don't usually talk about myself. I don't see the need for it. I would rather sit quietly and let the pageantry of each day parade before me, to be a witness to it all, that's enough for me, it's what I'm here for really. I feel it in the deepest part of me, not a religious fervor, but a fervor nonetheless. That and just, well, to be here for other people, that too, because it's in us to be that way, because even if other people can and will disappoint you most of the time, serving them is still something we must do. I'm ambivalent you could say. You can see that in me better than I can. I might want to believe we only have to take care of ourselves and those who depend on us, grit our teeth and find the pleasures that await us. But it isn't enough. We all need outside help, and it is an essential part of our nature to help others. To imagine people losing sight of that is to imagine the worst of outcomes for all people.

I do also make things. When I retired I attended classes in ceramics, enough to teach me what can be taught and then the rest has been a solitary road that I have loved for that very reason, and now I'm a potter. I work on an electric wheel in my own makeshift studio below our home. There is a dirt floor and exposed joists, more of a crawl space than a studio to be honest. I make my own clay and glazes. My pots, people say they are shapely and well made. Yes, they are well made, the clay of a regular thickness, the weight handy, quite light. I merely follow the possibilities I see in my mind's eye, and then they are baked in my electric kiln for the enjoyment and utility of whoever has them. I like making things, especially things that have a mouth at the top and a firm bottom, to give pleasure and to be vessels of containment. My glazes are green usually or brown, red that's copper-hued, everything subdued, the colors of autumn and evening, because I only came to this life in the winter of my days, even though this is work that requires some brute strength, a young man's craft. My shapes find themselves, and when a tea pot or a vase or even a cup is done I look at it in wonderment as I would if it had come perfect out of the earth, which of course it has, but only after passing through my hands and through my eyes. I try to interfere as little as possible. I don't impose myself on them, that's not how it goes, they find their own way through me. It's satisfying though. I don't know what it means to be an artist. I think I stop short of that, whatever it is. I find these objects that I have created, more in the way a creature waits for its prey to come out of hiding and then pounces. I don't create. I encourage and urge and nourish and after a few hours out comes a pot, and I can say I made that, but really it's more like I knew how to step back and stay out of the way and let it appear, with its own hunger and need, in terms of how it feels to me. And in the end I cannot say whether I am friend or foe of the things I make, I suppose I'm a bit of both. I wish I could put pictures here of my pots, in the same way as I can enshrine here these momentary passages and though they are mere words, momentary impressions, here they live and endure in a permanent way. Perhaps that will be possible, otherwise you'll have to guess just how strange and at the same time practical my pots are!

When Edith and I first come here, we're looking for a place to retire. We have already lived in New Mexico and could make a life for ourselves there, in the scorchingly beautiful nature of the southwest. But we have family here on this lake already. That is, Edith's sisters and a cousin have already congregated here. And so, we come and have a look. And what we find, out in the forest and on the lake, simply astonishes us.

The way the seasons are here means that there is always change in the air. The temperature of the water and the air is forever on the move, and with that the colors and even the rise and fall of the landscape. The shapes of streams and lakes are shifting constantly, even while, at the same time, they remain silent and still and unchanging. There is a primeval metamorphosing happening in every moment—a clearing returns to dense forest, and then in that same space the giants, the white pine, the great oak, maple and elm will take over from the first growth green ash, alder, poplar and birch. A stream bed will bloom into a wetlands and then become a pasture. Nothing moving, the lay of the land the same as it has been for hundreds of years at the same time as there is this churning.

Edith only paints still lifes. She's obsessed with the power of all these rooted life forms throwing out limbs and crowns of leaves, drinking in the light and the moisture, multiplying and rotting, the tender symphony playing, the sheer momentum and the scale. She loves ferns especially, which thrive in coolness and shadow, and the saplings that come seemingly from nowhere and grow quickly like the teenagers they are. The towering giants are more difficult for her to contain in her canvases until they fall, thunderously, and become, as they rot, like new mothers laying down their teats to fill the mouths of mushrooms and ferns, moss. The play of light on the water is never the same from one day or one hour to the next, affected by countless factors, from the time of day to the temperature and whether the sky is clear or overcast. In her watercolors it is always one particular moment. The unending kaleidoscope speaks to us, each sunset over the water different from the day before, or the new one to come tomorrow, no two the same. From the moment we arrive we're intoxicated with everything we see here.

I turn twenty-four in 1931, the worst year of the Great Depression. There's no work. I paint billboards across New Jersey. A friend of mine has a car, so they hire us. They give us paint brushes and cans of paint. They hardly pay us. We mostly earn our living giving rides to people for a few dollars, whatever they can afford, to bring them from one town to another. We paint the billboards too sometimes. The cash from the riders pays for our gas. It's not real work. You can't see yourself in it. Then I sell real estate, for pennies on the dollar. There are few buyers, but people are desperate to sell. These are terrible times. People are going hungry. The looks on their faces, decent people, not understanding, everything almost at a standstill. You learn a lot, and you learn a lot about yourself. I'm not in the game yet. I'm still too young for that. I have nothing to lose, but not much to gain either. You just want to survive. What's work? It's passing the time, not work in any meaningful way.

Edie and I are about the same age. I don't know what she sees in me, unless it's a reflection of the great admiration I feel towards her from the moment I set eyes on her. We're two skinny kids in our mid-twenties recovering from illnesses that might have killed us. There aren't many others our age there. We're sobered up by what we've been through, we both are, meaning we have this sense of the preciousness of what we have that was almost taken from us, not just our health but our entire futures.

I must be frank with you. I've said already that people are generally disappointing. We live with a paradise nested deep in our hearts, a place where people treat each other always with great forebearance and kindness and gentility, where adults are respectful towards the young, and where children do not simply respect and fear their elders but also play with them and understand (as children do!) that adults are children too. Always, always. And in our words, well, there are glimpses in our words of the paradise that exists within us. We express our ethics and our morals in words. But our actions are undermined by fear, because the world is a fearful terrain really. Fear is as corrosive as hydrofluoric acid, which I know a little about from working briefly in the oil extraction industry in Texas. Burns through metal and glass, breathing anywhere near it terribly toxic to the human organs. Our fears are real, make no mistake, and there is no such thing in us as fearlessness. But when you mix together our paradise and all too human fear what you get is hypocrisy and betrayal, plain stupidity, all the different human disappointments. If we could only be one of the dumber animals, things would be much easier and most people would be happy with that. Just feed and pet us, slaughter us from time to time if you must, but don't make us think, don't make us responsible for anything important. There, I can tell, you must be thinking I'm a misanthrope, and I guess I am. Don't count on people and you'll never be disappointed.

But in our case, Edith's and mine, it isn't some generalized thing, but rather certain very particular encounters we have with people we trust that hurts the most.

In the sanatorium, in the Adirondack Mountains region

near Saranac Lake in upper New York State, we live quite well and remain there for more than half a year together, getting to know each another. The place combines good meals and time outdoors with a healthy lifestyle that's rigidly enforced. No drinking, no smoking, nothing like that. Our doctors are guessers, innovators yes, but they're trying things out, and in those years there's no specific standard of care. Neither antibiotics nor vaccines are well understood yet, though they're being studied. It's known since the late 17th century that sometimes men suffering from tuberculosis improve after their lungs are pierced by swords in duels or in war, so there are also surgical treatments that are being tried. Our doctors decide to remove one of Edith's lungs, and we have no choice but to trust them. It's a terrible thing for her to have to go through. I feel they're playing at being Gods, our doctors, all while mostly being nothing more than fools in white coats. I hate them. And I think they mostly leave me alone because, like them, I'm a man and also perhaps because they realize I'm on to them. But I'm not able to stop them from doing what they did to Edith, and perhaps it saves her, I don't know. It may well have. Her case is worse than mine.

America has been many things to many people, a place of freedom, and a kind of torture chamber, let's be honest and say that it's never been just one thing or the other, that the freedom of some is always paid for by the penury of others. But here is something that is common in both extremes. It's always a place where you shed what you were to become something new. No longer Polish you're Polish American, no longer African you're African American. And it's a place of an almost grotesque plenitude. Remember that many people who arrive on these shores have seen starvation, or plague, drought, religious wars and wars of conquest. Here they find a sprawling continent of Indian nations and an extraordinary bounteousness, like none could have imagined possible—flocks of passenger pigeons in the millions and tens of millions, that are easy to kill and good to eat; in the West bison herds that cover tens of thousands of acres, in the north caribou populations equally unending. Salmon populations in the West and the East. There's no end to the natural richness, and this too mesmerizes people and inspires them with an idea of America as heaven on earth. Eventually, this deteriorates into a severe perversion of itself—American materialism and greed—but there is still somewhere here, or in us, that purer version of a place of great natural beauty and endless possibility.

I think when Edith and I turn our backs mostly on other people and become enamoured naturalists with full hearts, it's an expression of this—of these truths. Not everyone sees them. Some people, our friends, even see them in us. But for ourselves, every time we look out upon the waters of the lake, or whenever Edith goes off into the day with her portable easel and paints a tree stump or a bending stand of slender white birch saplings, she is as it were praying at the temple of nature, and comes home in the afternoon breathing the sheer elegance of what she has seen, and in her watercolors there's a prayerful silence of simple coexistence that we feel with these other life forms and all the ways they're harmonious with their surroundings, whether they're young or old and dying, whether bursting forth or rotting. The communication that we find between all the different life forms around us, the music of it, can be overwhelming. And though we move among it all carefully, pretending nothing much is happening, to us it's like we're carrying in us a secret of some dramatic happenings that we can barely keep to ourselves, this news of coronations and symphonies so loud and clamorous.

~

I think I told you already. When we're at the sanatorium in Saranac, New York, two young adults falling in love in the mountains, Edith's case is much more serious than mine. This is a long time ago now. But to me it could be the day before yesterday, so present is it in my mind.

Our doctors are powerful—and ignorant. That is, TB—consumption—has been killing people in droves for milennia—one-seventh of the world's population dies of it. And now, in only the last decade or so, there are vaccines, and antibiotics—new tricks in the medical bag. And most of all, fresh air, a return to nature, which is why these sanatoria are springing up all over the country, in mountainous regions but also in the desert, especially the high desert. But there's no science to it yet, no accepted standard of care. People are still dying, there's no cure. It's a free-for-all. And as with so many things, the real culprit, more than any other one thing is the lack of basic sanitation and nutrition and healthy living in that sense. I see all that now with 20/20 hindsight. Back then, well, as I say, we're in love, and we're sick, and don't know if we're going to die or live. I'm sure, though I don't really remember, that I want very much to live, but only if Edith is going to live, only if we will enter the future, our future, together.

As I have told you, the scourge that is tuberculosis isn't well understood yet. Medicine's main answer is fresh air! Because it has been shown to lead to better outcomes and to recovery in many patients. Our doctors have new tools, including vaccines and antibiotics, but no clear data to tell them in a scientific way which tools to use in which cases. So it's mayhem. Edith and I feel helpless in the situation. Our doctors in a certain sense must feel helpless also, or almost helpless. But they have authority. They're young, and the science of treating this awful disease itself is young. We all are. It's a terrible situation.

In Edith's case, they decide to remove one of her lungs, the one that's badly scarred, in the hope that in this way they will save the other lung and their plan is to do everything possible so that Edith's remaining lung recovers completely. She has to approve the plan. She doesn't like it. There's, honestly, savagery in it, human savagery, almost gleeful, warlike, it seems to us, I think, though we don't say so, not even privately between us. We look at them, ask roundabout questions. But to say no to their plan would be like an open revolt. We have no choice, really. It's like a morose game, a parade of falsity before a king that is death itself. So we say yes, or rather Edith does, saying we trust them, though we do not. And the surgery is scheduled.

Despite all our foreboding, the approach chosen by our doctors succeeds. Edith has the surgery, and the removal of the festering, collapsed lung eases her suffering. Recovery from going under the knife takes six weeks, but by the end she really is better than she was. The good lung is functioning more freely and its minor lesions heal. The tenderness between us is indescribable. We had no expectations really. We weren't playing the odds, we never asked our doctors what were the odds in her favor. No, we weren't thinking that way about it at all. Simply casting off, putting ourselves into the hands of others, not trusting them, but doing it anyway, not guided by hope or luck, nor by reason. We simply say to each other, this is one way forward and it is the path we are taking.

In those last days of our convalescence, our doctors request a meeting. We are leaving Saranac Lake soon, in two to three weeks. I remember that it's early springtime, still winter there where we are in the mountains, still winter in every sense, the snow drifts deep, the air still and the temperatures well below freezing, down into the teens some days and most nights, a kind of warm winter season on other days when the sun melts the top of the snow so that it shines like a body of water and you can already feel on the tips of your ears the warmer days that are coming in only a matter of weeks when it will all change and the green season will break through the white and gray one, when rushing water will be heard everywhere, something we haven't experienced in this place yet, since we've been here for less than a year.

I remember—Edith and I will both forever remember, with very mixed emotions—the meeting with our doctors and how it reveals something we find at the time to be quite shocking, or rather confusing, because we think it crosses a boundary in a way we find to be indecent, extending their investment in our—or rather in this case her, but also indeed our, since our destinies are now one—medical care to our future plans, our life plans in a way we feel is beyond their purview.

After they have examined Edith, a young doctor comes out to invite me into the examining room where Edith and I sit beside each other in adjoining chairs, holding hands, and three doctors stand across from us, one of them holding our files, their faces expressing their sense of fulfillment in a way that irks me. Gorden and Edith, they say, we have grown very fond of you and will be sorry to see you go. You have your whole lives ahead of you now, and can live them fully. The disease in you is on its way out, you're as cured as we can make you of the scourge of tuberculosis. We are very proud of how well you have both responded to our ministrations. We believe that the fullness in your hearts for each other has also contributed to your success. For us, it is very encouraging to see such a strong immune response, to see that this is possible when combined with healthy living in dry mountain air and good medical decisions.

It's strange because it's clear to Edith and me that this is all preamble to something else they want to say. And then it comes. With only one functioning lung and as thin as you are, as unprotected by fat as your vital organs are, you cannot have children. To do so might well kill you. It is not advisable. And in their eyes now that they have said it there's a curious light. Is it a sense of ownership? It is of course just one of the doctors who says this, but he speaks for them all.

So there it is, the betrayal. The road of clean living and abstinence leads to this, a kind of terrifying madness—healthiness to the point of strangulation of life and all the romance and danger that makes it worth living. We've both sensed it from the start. Behind the science and medicine there lies a cold calculation which has everything to do with control and suffocation.

What do we say in response? Edith nods her head and says nothing. I squeeze her hand and look away. I'm sure we've never talked about having children together before. It isn't on our minds at all. But from that moment, I think we both know we will. Their betrayal has given us a gift. Defiance grows strong in us from that moment. Together with the awareness that to do so will be dangerous to her—we don't doubt what they're saying. Along with seeing it as an absolute betrayal we just assume it's also more or less true. So right then the motivation is born of defiance and we know at least we will try. This makes us, well, it does not necessarily make her maternal or me paternal, but it makes us happy. Happy away from other people. We have our faith, our belief in God. And we see God in nature everywhere, in every leaf and stone and in the benefits of life that sunlight and rainfall bring. We see God also in chance, even in danger. We're comfortable putting ourselves in God's hands, we love God, quietly, but defiantly, one on one, unmediated really by the church we both belong to, which—even back then when we're in our twenties and the century is only in its thirties, is itself—our church—also young, founded only hundreds of years ago, and renegade in its origins. Very Protestant, or in our case, Episcopalian. But other people, even other churchgoing people, seem more and more to us like mishapen forms, fallen angels if you will. With some exceptions of course. But we do not assume the best of people. We wait, and trust in other things, and then we're pleasantly surprised sometimes. And I'd like to think we're always ready for that, for the pleasant surprises. We don't want to miss any. But the betrayal and, to us, interference, of our doctors affects us deeply. The meeting has been a signal moment in both our lives. Oh how we hate them, even if they've pointed us in the direction of an exhilarating path that indeed we walk together ever after.

Carolyn (1979)

I'm sitting up in bed in the big brown house just before first light, like I've arrived alone somewhere ahead of everyone else, the glowing bright dark coming through my two windows. It is as if our whole world were coming in for a landing at high speed among other spiraling, quickening worlds, all going at their own speeds in their own directions. The larger machine that encompasses all these colliding and rushing-by worlds is grinding away, universes dashing in different directions and even crashing into each other at the same time as it is completely still and quiet in the house.

A fullness in white appears in the center of the eastern sky, like a ghost, but small, just a button high up. Then, in reply, silhouettes start to appear in the field, modest building-block shapes of things, one by one. Then a tangle of them comes tumbling in, triangles, half-circles, diamonds and squares, but everything soft still and blurry, because there's almost no real light yet, just an invisible blackness everywhere. Then more light and more shapes, like two children playing, with one doing the most, pulling open the sky to let the light in, while the other tries to arrange everything in the proper order.

Over the next half-hour the light becomes huge, pressing down on the tree-tops, and the answer from below is more sharply defined. The funny part is, I come awake in the bat of an eye, while the world takes all this time to do its version of the same thing. And where you'd expect the solid earthly shapes to come forward in a broad wave, it doesn't happen that way. The opposite happens. As the light in the eastern sky grows in intensity, and broadens, like water rising now, here below individual figures step into the pre-morning one by one. A tall white pine along the driveway, then the shimmering and scrawny birch near the bottom of the field. Our car's windshield unexpectedly reflects a splinter of white light. Each of these still figures somehow steps forward and identifies itself here in the opening of the new day that is forever pure and untarnished in this moment. *Here I am, God*. All the shapes and colors appear unborn and eternal to me, without age. Everything so different from how it will be in the world only hours from now. And then, following these few first arrivals, other shapes enter in a rush, by the thousands now. Soon the day is fully formed and the door of the vault that holds the secrets is shut once more and hidden until tomorrow.

I sit by my window facing east, on the lookout for one of the small-dog-sized animals, a skunk or a porcupine, not night creatures but early morning ones, a groundhog or even a beaver. They will stick to the hems and seams of this still roughly sewn-together early morning, along the edge of the field where it meets the forest, or around the corner of our barn, feeling their way in the cool shadows there and sniffing more than looking, never crossing the open fields where an owl or hawk might find them. The early hour itself is a kind of pathway, these creatures like solitary pilgrims, their fur shiny with dew. And somehow it's apparent to me that they are so intent on what they're doing they don't realize that I can see them now. They still think they're under cover of night.

Then the whiteness and pinkishness that follows after the darkness disperses into itself. There comes an intense pale blueness, and then that also disappears. The silhouetted shapes of the trees turn mossy green now, while others are a white-gray, the color of mist, and still others light brown. But it is the blue sky and the mottled green field now that pull the day fully from the night, stringing it to the endless procession of similar days that have passed through here before, and to countless others that will follow.

I rise. If mama hears me she comes, wordlessly, like I've summoned her. Sometimes she is already up and I awaken to the small sounds of her industry downstairs, like she were stoking the day, pressing it forward, believing in it, the growing light out the windows a response to her urgings on. I come downstairs and stop halfway to sit on the stairs and in all the world there is only the two of us now. I watch her as she sets something slow-cooking on the stove, or kneads something on the cutting board, waiting until she looks up and sees that I'm here too. And then, on very good mornings, when we both have rested well during the night and there is truly nothing we need that we don't already have, she settles us together under a warm blanket in the corner chair with an open book where I fall back asleep with my eyes on her. I am seven, and she is just twenty-four. Between us, I am the oldest, no doubt about that, uninterrupted guide to her interrupted girl. Or we return upstairs together to her bed and sleep in now, even more deeply sometimes than during the night, holding each other in our arms, the daylight somehow like a doubling of the nighttime dark, the light covering the land like a blanket of snow and letting us be free of everything for a few hours more. Outside the dew burns off, the hours pass mostly in silence, the cards thrown down by the players at the end of every hand. Insects inspecting every inch of each one. Ferns, hastas, wild irises, and yellow pom-poms won't tell you what they're holding. The giveaways are the long grasses that sway and bend, the way you sometimes see pregnant women do, one hand on their bellies, the other on their brows. This isn't a rain forest, and yet it is a teeming borderline between our humankind with our ways and the forest and mountain creatures and theirs. Which is wilder? Ours is. Which more changeable? If you mean in harmony with its surroundings, it is impossible to say. Which older? Most of the animals and plants among us here are young, or youngish, and the ways of people old and decrepit. There are exceptions though. There are creatures here that express an ancientness far beyond ours, land tortoises and also the sullen brown snapping turtles with heads that look only half-finished they are so old, and the loons of course. They're here back with the dinosaurs, and somehow survive the ice ages, and the glaciers passing through, the slowest dance of all.

With the rising sun still low on the mountain ridges across the open water and the day not too hot yet, we set up our beach chairs in the shallows, poking our toes underwater into the granular sand that's not native to this place or really alive at all the way everything else here is. She sits me on her knees and basts us both with Bain de Soleil from the Five and Dollar, both of us sleepy, doing absolutely nothing on principle because nothing is the one thing that will never come undone or be taken from us. Sunscreen glistens in little ribbons on the water, sunfish nibble our toes, a goldfinch and a starling ricochet overhead, the day still very young, the sun as it touches us still soft like a furry paw. We've stolen a march on the lumbering day. The continuous lines of ourselves are unnaturally long and graceful when we get up and high-step into the water to cool off, the flat top of the lake bone dry, our top halves and our bottom halves making a sideways "z," the lake water somehow congealing into a goo that sticks to your fingers like marshmallow.

By noon all the magical queerness has burned off in the heaviness and the heat, the weight of the day now as factual as a car wreck, but by now we've slipped away, reclaimed the house with its tinny coolness, and for another hour or two we still wear our laurels in the stillness of the hour. Ahead of us in the afternoon and evening still to come we see open vistas filled with endless possibilities. After lunch we rest again, together upstairs in one of our beds or apart, in the near dark again indoors, the house still cool even on the hottest summer days. Until finally the near mountain west of us steals the gentle afternoon sun away before its time, and we find ourselves adrift and doomed again. How those feelings always have a kind of permanence to them, while the lighter-hearted ones seem impermanent and fleeting even always.

Mama says the absence of the late afternoon sun is something she'll never be able to get used to. But I'm comforted by how early and uneventfully the darkness comes, the peacefulness and the easiness of the loss. There's only before and after, only daylight and then its absence, followed later on by the incredible starry night we usually have out here, that surrounds and envelops us like an ocean around a small island, around and around, all the minor notes blending together and then the general stillness and quiet that comes, impossibly, countlessness pulsating, the living things of the night vibrating with their own comfort and communion, which includes us. We're denizens now in the dormancy, the waiting of every cool and star-filled night. Above me the aurora borealis is like a bright mist. I can see through my windows a thick brush of orange and yellow and purple light. It's funny how some of the things that distress mama the most I find comforting. I'm not tortured by hopes and disappointments the way she has been. What captures me are the enduring things and I accept our greivances more easily than she does. I don't know why.

When the moon rises, the house ties itself to it. After the sickness of our long, sunless, late afternoons when the mountains hide the sun, the unsought after moonlight can be as near and intimate as someone standing beside you holding a candle in each hand. Our three chimneys and the steeply pitched rooves draw in the white light so that it covers us like a veil. By our tinyness the neverending universe above is measured and recorded. Amen. And being out on such nights under the eye of a nearly full moon is like accompanying ourselves across our dreams.

When Jennie and Marie are here, sometimes Marie and I come outside after dinner to sit on the porch steps to wait for the moon to rise. We hold hands or wrap our arms around each other. Not talking, looking out as the visible world drifts away. First there is the pageant of the dragon flies and the bats, the dragon flies first, the bats joining in. It's the Feast of the Mosquitoes! We hear the bullfrogs, and then the murmurs of mama's and Jennie's voices from inside, the percussion of confession, or the rippling laughter, and then the moon comes out of the treetops, more or less suddenly, pearly white, and on its shoulder the dancing north star, and then other stars, small and flashing.

Mama only has two points of reference. One is me, the other is Jennie. Since mama is the oldest of us three, there is a burden in her that we cannot remove and she cannot share. One eye is always on us. On Jennie, wherever she may be, and on me, and her other eye on her own eventual escape. She'd have left already, but for her daughter and her sister—and we are both of us her daughters *and* her sisters—but we only keep her here for now. Like my grandmother, she is someone who stays for awhile and then saves herself by leaving.

Other summer mornings we want fresh softboiled eggs with toast, and we abandon our cold house for the short walk up the road. She carries me the last part of the way and puts me down at Agnes's broken asphalt driveway, and I open the white screen door that leads directly into her kitchen. If she's not there already, Agnes hears us and comes around, glad to see us. We sit at her kitchen table, looking out on the road and the field across the way, while she goes off to the barn in search of eggs.

I sit in Agnes's wicker chair and after a few minutes she reappears, turning the eggs over in the bruised open half-carton. And they are perfect—small, in different mottled shades: salt and pepper, cloud white, coffee-with-cream off-white, darker or lighter, splotched sometimes with a little hen shit, still warm.

Once mama asks to see her layers, and Agnes politely refuses, saying she doesn't want to disturb them again so soon.

Back home we boil the eggs for three minutes on a timer, one each or two each depending on our mood. I make the toast and butter it, which she then cuts into finger-wide strips that we set out on the plate on either side of the egg cups. I scalp one with a knife, revealing the bright liquid fire of the yolk. I add salt, dip the strip of toast in, and taste the sweetish blood and sunlight of the egg in my mouth. Mama does the same after me. We're quick and efficient. As we take our first bites, we look into each other's eyes. She rolls hers. I make believe to swoon. We sip our sweet, hot, milky, orange pekoe tea. Ashland slips away like an iceberg sinking into the ocean. Sometimes mama even gets talkative on such mornings, lightheartedly, in a way I don't see her do often.

The women in our family have always been swimmers. At the river house, Jennie and mama continue that tradition, the pull of the current notwithstanding. Most days at the big brown house, in the summer but also in the spring and the fall, mama swims. She goes on her own. Just disappears. Or I accompany her to the water and on those days, when we wander down the path to the beach together, me carrying our towels, there's a stealthiness in her, like she's looking for her chance to escape with every step. And the whole story of our closeness changes in this hour as she becomes a more forceful version of herself, and I can be more childlike. The reshuffling can be the temporary making right of us, or just a wrongness between us.

She suits up under her towel like a woman with a purpose, wades into the lake, and dives under the low morning sun, diamonds flashing off the surface all around her. Swimming out she's a different person now. How a seamstress sews on her electric machine, the pedal propelling the cloth forward with an invisible insistence, mama burrowing into the thick coat of the lake is like that, entering the far-off picture of sky and sun, green mountains and black water, never turning to look back at our little sandy beach or me.

I feel myself getting smaller and smaller the further away she is. I ask myself, *Why doesn't she just keep on going?I would if I were her.* She reaches the bend and is gone. I stand where I am, still as a statue, holding our towels, desperately lonely and cold all of a sudden. I change as quickly as I can into my own clammy swimsuit, put on my orange life preserver, dip my toes into water that feels alive now in an uninviting way, and become almost paralyzed, as if I've been defeated already by all these minuscule trials. After a while I enter the frigid water, let it invade me, and then swim a little, bobbing along in my undignified orange life preserver, just to our floating raft, where I climb up and wait for her. The emptiness of the scene without her is like an angry crowd arrayed against me. I close my eyes to be alone with my afraid self, a lesser harm it seems to me right then than to be brave but no less alone.

Now suddenly she's next to me in the water, her elbow on the raft. Her hand touches my foot, her earned smile and below it the brace of her shoulders taut, her breaths coming in short passes, hair shining, auburn curls pressed to the sides of her temples. I look at her and see how filled she is with anticipation. I all but don't recognize her as my mother now. And then in her smile I see that in this moment she is thankful for me again, grateful to me simply for letting her swim, for releasing her as in fact truly I did do. For a moment we're both free and I share her relief. But then the foreboding returns to me. I gaze at her, hurting with my love, filled with nothing but heartbreak, the knot that never is loosened. This version of mama that I respect and admire is the woman who will go, and the version that will always be mine is the broken-into-pieces girl who will never be this woman.

There was a time when her whole life to come spread out before her like a beautiful landscape. That's always here. It is the landscape of her face now. So nothing changes. She is my genie, I am her denier. I remember something Jennie said to me about river swimming: *You go in knowing you can drown. It only has to happen once. And the water is far stronger than you are. Girls drown all the time. But every time we swim in the river we get stronger and it's a little safer than the time before. And in the end we're pretty safe, and usually the person who goes in and drowns is some newbie, not one of us.* Mama looks safe to me swimming out, the dangerous part for her is returning. I'm thankful now because she's here beside me again. My crazy thoughts fade away. I look down at her and touch her arm that lies beside me on the raft, thankful even as I see a part of me break away, paralyzed and rooted here, and forever unfree. That's us in a nutshell, mama and me, both of us free but not free of each other.

We hear Jennie's car come up and then the welcome rat-a-tat of the slamming doors. She holds her lower back and stands crookedly, Marie and Ed are rolling on the grass. It's like our dogs are returning. They're wild, but more ours than anyone else's. The return of our strays, who let us out too when they're here, unlocking something in us. When Jennie and the kids are here, mama and I know everything is in its rightful place, and without them we never feel that way. We're not strays like they are, but we're never not drowning here, and there is something Jennie cannot do for herself that she does for us.

Andy comes with them now some of the time, in Jennie's car or in his own truck right behind them, and once we recover from the shock of his presence, we're soon in over our heads with him too, in the same way I imagine Jennie is. He's a local man but not like local men are usually. That is, he is hard the way they all are, quiet, brooding—but there's a spark in him. He's funny, and when are Ashland men ever funny?

She is made of stone and he is a basket woven around her, strong too. Stone and basket don't mesh or blend. They're too different. But they can complement each other amazingly. He's a little shy, a little menacing, and he is not just some guy she's seeing, he's Marie and Ed's—and soon-to-be Harold's—father! Even so, he's only a resident in their lives, a roomer. I don't know how I know, but it's obvious, and no one contradicts that idea. I never feel Andy owns any part of them or their lives. This is Jennie's way. You have to abide by it. He makes babies with her, and knows his responsibilities. But even as young as I am I understand that this is how she wants it and at the same time that he isn't enough for her. A few nights a week Jennie brings Marie and Ed to us so she and Andy can be together just the two of them. Mama's in charge and I'm her second-in-command. And when Jennie comes the next morning to get them, the look on her face is ever, Don't ask me to explain what I don't understand myself.

Andy has the very thrilling green eyes of a saint. I'll grant him that. And pink scars on his face and neck from an old tractor accident that somehow only adds to his beauty. And his sour-funny personality, that also only adds. He moves in a slow-funny steady way and is graceful. I know Jennie really loves him and I know she doesn't love him as he deserves to be loved. I'd marry him if I were old enough, and I'd be with him in a way that would make him happy, to hell with Jennie! He is perfect so far as I am concerned. But I don't blame her. She is blessed by the love of a good man, and cannot accept it.

Mama says, He loves a woman who can't help herself, and his suffering only makes this boy more beautiful. He doesn't draw strength from Jennie, she adds, and I'm only a kid but even I know you have to make your beloved stronger.

I have a paradise in me. I think everyone does, where everything is right and stands in a right relationship to every other thing.

Being eight is only a sideways step from being seven. I'm not getting older, just a little longer. In the same way as July is a little longer than June. But since I'm starting to look older, people leave me to myself more. I take up space differently from how I used to. I hear my own voice more clearly, and even the soft noises I make that don't mean anything, I hear them more clearly now too.

I spend more time writing and drawing. When I look at something, it never says just one thing to me. And what I do is never what I thought I was going to do, it's always completely different from what I thought it would be. I like that about myself and my work.

Knowing so well all the things that aren't possible helps me accept what is, which is only the element of surprise. I look at my pictures sideways sometimes. My feelings are safe in them.

I think I'm starting to understand the natural world that lives in Edith's paintings and in Gordon's pots, this paradise of mine is not a lonely one, anyone who does this is there, people of all ages tending to paradise.

~

Mama has brown eyes, Jennie's are a distant blue. Jennie's taller and has shapelier ears than mama. Mama—even in her young adult life—has been altered by her experiences, whereas Jennie, Jennie, no, not in any way that I can see. In my child's mind's eye I make lists of the differences. Two sisters who both like to tell me they don't understand each other at all. Mama brags to Jennie about some brave thing she does, someone she stands up to. Jennie tells us how nice she is to someone. But mama is never brave in public and Jennie isn't comfortable with being a nice person.

Mama and I don't have a lot freedom of movement. We're planted, like trees. Our freedom is just a freedom to grow and not be ruled by anyone. Jennie is ruled by Jennie and she is a tyrant. And though she would not want to be thought of as kind, God knows she is kind to mama and me.

Mama and Jennie communicate with looks and with their hands, by word and sign. They've dated some of the same boys, mama still goes out with this one or that one. So their love lives aren't private and are a favorite topic when Andy's not here, their hands and bodies moving in the telling, all mischief. A kind of power lives inside them.

I am jealous of their closeness, how when Jennie doesn't come for a week or more, mama can fall into a pit of loneliness even though I am right here beside her. But then she comes, and mama relents and looks at me, glad I'm near her now that Jennie is back.

~

I've reached a stage in life where everything is funny. Andy and Jennie are going to get married. I think that's pretty funny. Especially since Jennie is being disagreeable about it.

He wants to marry me, is all she says to mama and me, speaking with more regret in her voice than she should have. Then she adds, Finally. And even, Thank God. Not meaning to be funny. But after she says that, mama and Jennie laugh until they cry. Mama comes over and picks me up. I'm heavy for her to carry, now that I'm eight, so it's special when she does it. I watch Jennie from her arms and, like they're noticing me for the first time, the two of them see me staring at them and start to laugh and cannot stop. Ed and Marie come over. We all start dancing around the kitchen, all five of us.

~

It is mid-June and what's wrong is just that nothing feels any different. Mama is the same, but there's a weight on her that's new. It is the quietest suffering you could ever imagine.

Around this time my grandmother comes out to see us finally, my father's mother, one of the first times she does. Jennie and Andy being about to get married probably has something to do with it. There is hurt in her eyes standing on what used to be her porch, or maybe just tiredness. But we're happy to see her and proud she's come. We sit outside at the picnic table, and mama brings coffee for her and tells her all about it. We even ask her to come back for the wedding, knowing she won't. I show her my drawings and some poems. I see she can't pay attention to anything, so I put them aside and hold her hand, and she lets me. She closes her eyes, feeling close to me I can tell, letting me be her island, the daughter of the son who went away never to return.

After she leaves, mama waits awhile, like she were deciding what to say to me about the visit, then what she actually says is, If she ever lets herself feel one regret there'll be no end to all the regrets she will have to let herself feel.

And, I guess that when her son leaves us she doesn't understand at first he's leaving her too.

I let myself wonder about that. How can he leave us and never come back? I understand our side more or less perfectly, not the words of course, but just what losing something is like. That, and mama's pride which is also mine by extension. But I cannot begin to understand a boy who becomes free of encumbrance so easily. It sounds horrible to me, a worse torture.

This is the year the bullfrogs disappear. In the year when we arrive they are so loud during the first summer months, their breeding season, that at night the deep bellowing that rises up from the lake to the house shakes the nighttime sky to its earthbound foundation, not ominous nor mysterious exactly, just insistently announcing itself, over and over. There are choruses where countless bullfrogs erupt together and sometimes a single croaking that one animal emits at regular intervals. To me it sounds like another, *I am here, Lord.* I remember closing my eyes and imagining being one of them. They don't know death in the way that we do, I realize. They come and go. They aren't sentimental about it as we are. And then suddenly this year, they're gone. Not a peep. No trace of them.

Marie and I wear matching dresses for the wedding, like twins. They give us a minor role in the ceremony and in preparation for it mama gives us lessons in how to say nothing and do nothing, which she calls being "poised." Our dresses and shoes are red with pink straps and ribbons. We decide that the longest we can be poised for is five seconds. Somebody else says that to complain about us, but we agree. Five seconds is a long time, we say.

Uncle Andy whoops and chicken-runs after us across the fields whenever he sets eyes on us, puffing out his chest with his hands holding his suspenders and flapping his elbows. Then he lopes coyote-style back to where Jennie is, where everyone sits in chairs that fan across our front field and we sneak back behind him making faces. Edward runs after us breathlessly wherever we go. Sometimes he stops to have one of his tantrums—he's losing ground on all sides, with little Harold in Jennie's arms most of the time now, and Andy and Jennie getting along. So Marie and I settle around him cooing and fussing like the little mothers of his dreams.

It is a happy day. Andy and Jennie are our king and queen. She is twenty-two, and he is thirty. They are beautiful together, and it all spills over to Marie and Edward and Harold and me like a light shower that makes us forever beautiful too.

Harold is exactly five weeks old the day of Jennie's wedding, sleeping in a cradle that lies on the ground besides mama, who rocks it with her foot. Jennie comes over frequently to look at him, the extreme sleepy closeness between them stretching over us like a giant billowy sail.

Jennie wears a simple white cotton summer dress that the aunts made for her, with a little riot of embroidery in a rainbow of colors at the neck and the hem and the cuffs, and real flowers in her hair and sandals on her feet. She looks like herself, but as if Ashland were a mountain town in the Urals or on the Baltic Sea. Her skin is soft and radiant, and if she is our queen today she is a kind and benevolent one. When Jennie had Marie she was only fourteen years old, a child but one who knew exactly what she was doing, protected by mama on one side and by Andy on the other. Today she's twenty-two, a mature young woman who has everything she needs to be happy and to share that with those who depend on her.

But we're not enemies of death. I can look into the quietness in her eyes and it is a little pot she is stirring, a mixture of love and pain. I don't know why exactly, but I can see everything that's coming. And if I am crying all of a sudden with happiness, I am also seized with terror at what I'm seeing. Marie comes laughing to me, and holds me in a tight embrace from behind, thinking it's just happiness that I'm feeling.

We race across the slow-moving fields after dragonflies. And then we walk up the aisle between the rows of chairs, following Andy and Jennie, with their rings clasped tight in our hands, and holding each other's other hand. Kindly Mrs. Mills is doing the honors as mail-order justice of the peace. We stand to one side like we're supposed to. Jennie and Andy are wed and now the silver rings are on the ring fingers of their left hands and they have their kiss. Jennie smiles at us now and for just a little while she is shy and a child again with no responsibilities, which is the happiest part for her. And then everyone comes to congratulate Andy and Jennie both for really doing it, like they have won against all odds, and they really have, even I can see it.

Now everyone's gone. Mama has Marie, Ed, and Harold in the house. I'm walking over to Gordon and Edith's, who left right after the ceremony. As I go down our road, the field in shadow, the treetops painted yellow by the last rays of the sun, the sky showing three coats of blue as thick as black, all of it fading fast, I tiptoe off one foot onto the other, trying to keep my balance. If I tried to describe this day it would take me a hundred years, a hundred thousand pages. All the different parts and viewpoints. How many lifetimes would I need really even just to describe one minute of this day? More, more lifetimes than I could count. Even just thinking of Edith, just her alone, sitting on her chair in the field, holding Gordon's hand, remembering their wedding let's say. How they began their life together against all odds, inspired by that, their defiance the expression of their love! And now watching Jennie and Andy do it.

~

After being married barely five months, Jennie decides to call it quits. She comes to talk to mama first. They sit in the corner of the dining room talking quietly so we cannot hear.

Another day Jennie comes over to tell us Andy still wants to give her the house. He isn't trying to get me back, she says. Says in a loving way, like looking over her shoulder at someplace beautiful she's leaving behind. He knows this time we're parting for good. He loves me enough to let me go, she says, then adds, So our marriage isn't exactly a failure, just something that happened.

One day all of a sudden I realize that Marie, the word Marie, is a me with an ah in the middle. And the next time we're all together Marie and I decide that two daughters of two sisters are sisters too.

Jennie has a job interview at the golf course over by the next lake past ours. She wants to show us her new look. She has her nails and her hair done. She looks totally different—younger and older at the same time. She wants us to see the spectacle she's made of herself.

She says, I decided not to look for work in Ashland.

And as she laughs the way she always does, the individual strands of her new hair helmet are shaking. Mama and I both stare because we just can't get enough of her. It's as if she's been away for years living in another country and somehow returns to us transformed and yet unchanged, the greatest of miracles.

Part Three

Geoff (1992)

Failure's always interesting. Interesting—what do I mean by that? More human?

I'm a professor—or more literally an assistant professor, but tenure-track—of writing. I *profess.*

Many real writers also teach, but it's less common for real teachers, even professors, to also have writing careers.

I'm a teacher of creative writing, and a failed writer myself. That's very common—a stream with many tributaries, one being that as a failed writer I need a way to earn a living, and another that as someone who takes my job seriously and pours myself into it, I have less time and energy left for my own writing.

If I were a full professor I might have no more than two classes per semester, one or two. But as an assistant, I teach five, sometimes six. That's a lot of work—all so that the full professors can carry a lighter load.

Failure, success, these are abstractions, concepts. But the loneliness of failure isn't abstract, it's real. I know. The loneliness of success? I'm sure that's real too. But how interesting could it be?

So Plymouth State isn't Columbia. Not a lot of English majors, not a lot of people who know a second language. Now that I've been here some years, I can go even further into this idea: I have come to love the state of New Hampshire. I really mean that. Love. But it is not a state with a written culture to speak of. A lot of writers live here actually. They come here to write their books. But that's carpetbagging. And of course everyone in New Hampshire knows how to read. It's not a Third World country. But like some countries I can think of, this is a state with a tough and generous beauty in the soil and in the character of the people too, and nowhere is that written down.

If you want to understand New York and it's people, go read Edith Wharton. You can read James Fennimore Cooper for God's sake. Walt Whitman, and Melville. James Baldwin, Ralph Ellison. The list is nearly endless and after a while you'll understand New York and its people. But if you want to feel the pulse of the granite state you must climb her mountains, you must taste the water, you must let in the rockiness and the cold. There's never been a writer that captures this in books. In the 19th Century they're all from Massachusetts and Connecticut. Sarah Orne Jewett's from Maine but she's an exception.

New Hampshire is an uncouth state. The written language is used for receipts and bills of sale, for local historical society bolderdash. The people are a people of few words. To me, that makes them more, not less, writerly. But that's me. In the 20th century there's Robert Frost. He was changed by his time in New Hampshire and did his best work here, poems about the land and the life here. Then there's May Sarton, and I like her a lot. A tough lesbian, and eventually she quit the state and moved to Maine. But she has the New Hampshire grit. Born in Ghent in Belgium, her father taught at Harvard, she lived in different places, but longest in New Hampshire and here was where she learned the sound of her own voice. I suppose I'm picking and choosing, but to me she's a real New Hampshire writer—one of the few—who helps me understand this state and its people.

I like it here. The nearness of the Whites—America's tallest peaks east of the Mississippi—lends to every class I teach something I don't think is to be found anywhere else, though I might not be able to put it into words—and maybe that's just the point—an otherness, another-place-ness that cannot be put into words.

There are two main groups of students here at the college, two major parties if you will, the drinkers and the hikers. We're a small college, but we're in the top-ten of the nation's best drinking schools—not the state, the nation. And then of course there are the hikers, lanky kids who can scale Eisenhower, Washington and Adams in a single day—in sneakers! Their feet don't actually touch the ground, the way they do it. Gazelles. This is a state of many miracles, but they aren't in the writing arts. And Plymouth State is a college of many miracles too, one of which is that you can go to your morning class and still get on one of the forty-eight 4,000-footers before lunch and be back in your dorm in time for dinner.

I help my students put the right word in the right place. That is the closest thing in the world to doing nothing. It's not creative, and it's not earth-shaking and it's all I'm capable of. If you're writing something, I might be able to help you by teaching you something of what I know about what words are and how they act. It might be next to nothing, but it isn't nothing. It's just looking where you wouldn't normally look. And at the same time, helping you lay claim to something that's yours already. I know something about how to do that. I want to be useful, and I'll tell you if I think I can be. It's a huge privilege, to be honest. Not many people have the skills that I do in this area, maybe no one else does. It's fueled by a kind of starvation inside me. Were it not for that, I would not have the strength to do what I do as a writing professor, day in day out.

I'm not in it for flattery or fine talk. I'm a nuts and bolts guy, a plumber or a mechanic. Writing is physical work. Labor. That's what I believe. Not fine furniture-making or psychology. We all use words. They're survival tools. We use them to avoid misunderstandings and to control our own behavior and sometimes to control the behavior of others. They are powerful weapons, or can be. They can be hurtful, especially when they are harnessed to tell the truth with harmful intentions, because remember it isn't truthfulness that matters, it's why you're saying it.

What makes teaching writing difficult is that what we do in this class is to disabuse ourselves of the obvious power words have. My intention is to free words, to do *less* with them, that's probably the main thing. You don't heal or effect change by building them up, you accomplish those things by letting them say less.

For example, in the same way that I am interested in failure, I am also interested in repetition. Repetition is normally assumed to weaken, to attenuate, the power of words. But does it?

There's not much out there that isn't repetition of one form or another. But if we can add human intention, let's say, then—embrace of opposites—repetition can be its own antidote. A repeated word can have an entirely new meaning or purpose. That's if you do it right, and that's where the art comes in. It's always about doing it just right.

When I first move up here, I have a wife and kids. But I come here alone. My wife keeps her job, we keep our home for her and our kids. I go back when I can. Once I'm here and start working, I notice something. I notice it in the same way as when you're so surprised by something someone says, you ask them, Can you say that again please? It's that people up here don't make remarks about other people as much as I'm used to hearing people do back where I come from. I'm not hearing people talk about good people and bad people, or even about happy lives or unhappy ones and I'm so glad that's the way it is here. You all are so lucky to be from here. Now, it could be New Hampshire people are just generally so suspicious up here in the north country that they don't have any particular prejudice against some people more than others. There's an independent spirit that favors no one. Even in Church. I'm Episcopalian, so I go down to Ashland on Sunday mornings if I go anywhere. Churches aren't the same everywhere, and I've been to ones in other states where there's hate speech. But not up here. People up here seem to me to be a bit more private than they are in other places where I've lived, but I think it's also that nature humbles us all in this northern part of the state and teaches us manners in its own way. Or maybe it's not manners, but morals. What with the cold up here, the savagery of nature up here sometimes, we all get to look inward a good amount and know better than to point a finger at anyone else. I've been here nearly twenty years. I know I still seem like I'm from somewhere else, but the truth is that by now I'm more New Hampshire than not.

And to finish the thought, after the first two years I don't have a wife anymore, and when the kids have to choose they say they don't know me. And they're right. Without realizing it at the time, I've left Earth, almost like an astronaut, and landed in New Hampshire with no way back.

I have one student, a local kid from Ashland, the mill town just south of Plymouth. She's been coming to my classes for four years, since high school. She sits there glaring at the college kids. Her life, what I know of it, is a real mess. I don't try to help her. She's not a charity case. She's a strong person. I have nothing but respect for her. I don't really crit her efforts. She knows what she's doing. There's no goal or intention that I can discern, no ambition either. She just writes. That's all she does.

Not to make anything better by it. Just to keep a record of what is seen and done, both the parts she understands and the parts she doesn't. To me, she's a miracle as a writer. And my role as her writing teacher, most of the time, is just to read, to bear witness in that way to the record she keeps of the things that happen to her. Her presence in my class adds immeasurably to what it means to me to be here doing what I do.

I'm known as a hard grader, that's my reputation at the college, most kids stay away from my classes and I'm glad they do. I'll flunk you if you don't show up for class and do all the homework. I'll never flunk you though for any other reason. I will not judge you, or grade you based on whether I like your writing or not, only on the intensity of your commitment to what you're doing. So the kids that sign up and take my class are kids that actually want to write, or they just don't know what they've gotten themselves into and those kids drop the class in the first week.

Andy (1981)

When Jennie has Marie at fourteen, I'm 22, eight years older. It's 1972. You can say it's irresponsible, but you'd be wrong. I know she can count on me. We're not horsing around. We're building a life together. Three years later, at 17, she has Ed, so I'm 25—working, working. And sleeping hard. Our small world like a tree on the hillside soaking up the sun all day long, and dreaming through the cold dark nights. We don't have a plan, but everything's working out as if we did.

I'm working all the time, but not for myself. I'm working for Jennie and Marie and Ed. Nothing in my life ever felt as good as this does.

Then last year, 1980, she has little Harold, and a few months later we finally get married. She's 23 now, in this holy year of 1981. I'm 31. And we just got divorced. Not five months married, she tells me she's sure she does *not* want to be my wife. I'm angry when she tells me. I'm still angry now. There's no reason to tear us down. But, Godammit, I swear I still trust her to know what she's doing, and so I agree, fool that I am. No one knows where it's going to end.

Our best year was 1975. I'm still living at home with ma and pa. Jennie and the two little ones are living on River Street with the aunts. I'm saving between $500 and $1,000 a month, honest to God I am, sometimes I sock away $1,500, every penny goes into the bank, investing in our future, Jennie's and mine. We drop off the kids with Ellie and go around in the truck, my left arm on the wheel and my right for us holding hands, or wrapped around her shoulders so she can lean into me, king and queen surveying our domain. In the spring, new branches like bright green pencils standing up come off the old ones, and in the fall it's the red apples set against the orange and red and brown of the turning leaves of the forest behind them. Rows upon rows of apple trees marching across the fields for as far as the eye can see. Wild turkeys roam in flocks of five or twenty-five or more, like kids on a school outing. Maybe a deer eating apples off the ground that looks up at us, a tremor passing through her, not even a little afraid of us. We look for houses that might be for sale, making a game of it. Jennie tells me why the school in one town might be better for the kids than the school in a different one. She's happy with me. Some days I don't hardly say a word, which is fine with me. I may be older and wiser, but she's the one in charge. After my ma, there's Jennie. That's about it for me. My pa, my big brother before he got hurt and me aren't moved out of our chairs by much. Things that need doing speak to us and we listen. Besides that it's only ma, and even with her mostly we don't listen, but when she needs us to we do. I learn everything from pa: You only listen when you have to.

Ma is hungry for me, her second-born son. Not in a selfish way, more *questioning*. I'm her own blood, but at the same time it is as if she doesn't know where I came from. I'm what she knows but that's not all. What she's missing, I would have said, the part of my self that ma can't make heads nor tails of, is the part that belongs to Jennie. But then Jennie is just the same! She also only feels she can understand me up to a point. She's hungry for me too, but not selfishly enough, I'd say. Instead she is just kind of a little curious about me and who I really am. I don't understand these things I'm relating, even though I can see them plainly and clearly, in ma and in Jennie. Let's say they're cynical people, I'm not saying they are, but let's say so. Then the thing they see in me is something that goes against that. It's some kind of goodness they see. But they're wrong if they think most men don't have it.

A lot of boys around here enlist right from high school when they turn 18, or 19, or 20. Some do not return. Others come home hurt, which is exactly what happens to my own brother. Hurt pretty bad, caught up in the machinery of that war. There are also the girls that leave the state and are not heard from again. And that seems to us in mysterious ways like a war also. Just how it goes, a certain number of casualties being how the overall plan stays on course, kind of like the March of Civilization that we learn at school. We accept that some young people who don't have all that much of a future anyway die or just get taken out of the action in one way or another. There was a time when every young person growing up here was needed here and belonged. There was work enough farming the land, in the timber trade, good jobs, and in the mills too. You could find a house, raise a family, take care of your parents when they were old and infirm. That was the rhythm here, and it lasted for many generations. It's gone now, just gone.

There's the war in Vietnam the same years that the wool and paper mills in Ashland are winnowing down to almost nothing. The less work there is the more our boys enlist. There were five hundred mill jobs in Ashland once. It's dwindled down to seventy-five, and then to none. No paper and no wool blankets or gloves are produced here anymore. The machines were sent to other countries. Logs from our forests are strapped onto 18-wheelers and taken to sawmills in other states or the few New Hampshire ones that are still going. And I will say that the lesson isn't lost on any of us that things can end sooner rather than later, that you can go off to war and no one around here will tell you don't go. Even if we do say it, it's with a certain look that says, Even if you make it back alive after your tour of duty in Vietnam, what will you do for work?

All the things that used to need to be done here, and needed all hands on deck to do—the care of the fields and the orchard trees, the planting, the weeding, the uprooting, the care of the livestock, the fence post hole digging, the harvesting, the tapping and cooking down of the maple syrup—we helped with all of it. With the work. We knew who we were and we weren't bothered about it. You should have seen the corn fields here, how it was. Tall all summer long, taller than a man by summer's end. And on the hills rows and rows of apple trees like a conquering armada on surging seas.

But then it got to be that there was less work. They didn't need us to help like they used to because there was so much less of it. Almost no corn, less meat that was local, less of everything. The older people had barely enough for themselves to do.

So much of the land was sold off, piece by piece, a few acres at a time to pay the taxes. The hundred-acre farm, and that was not an unusual size for a family farm back when I was coming up, would get whittled down in one generation. The smaller the farm is the less it produces and the more of it you have to sell the next year to make ends meet. In our family, what was left still kept ma and pa busy, moving from dawn to nighttime almost. But there was less and less they needed me for as the size of the farm kept receding like melting ice, and from time to time they'd sell another small parcel for one reason or another. Then in the end they sold the rest, the house and barns and all, and moved into a mobile home on a nice plot of plantable land right on the banks of the Pemigewasset on the other side of

Ashland. And I swear to you they like living there better than in the old house, since everything is new and there's very little trouble to keeping that household going.

Mostly, that work, farming? It's gone now. You don't see a tractor pulling a hoe across a field to carve a furrow much anymore. There's hard work still, clearing the new growth at the edges of the fields for example, to keep the forest at bay. But that's mostly it. Holding on for dear life to what's still here so we don't lose that too. Farming, now? A few token things, to keep the memory alive, I guess, of how it's done. But it's not the engine of this part of the world as once it was. The glimmer that's still left is in us, in our selves, the memory of what everything was like when this land took everything we had and gave back to us in equal measure what it took from us.

I remember everything. Not just how it was for us kids, but how the life was, the way the men walked, the strength in them, the look in their eyes when they looked out onto the fields and to the end of the fields at the forest. And most years they'd be *adding* land, reclaiming land from the forest, taking down tall pine and elm and maple and oak and pulling out the stumps, and the soil would be rich because it hadn't been farmed in a hundred or even two hundred years sometimes. Before that, it was all fields around here I'm told, or mostly field anyway. Your fields along the road touch up against the next neighbor's fields, with only the low stone wall to mark the boundary, where now there are acres of wood and the remaining fields are like jewels, but mostly it's woods not field, with the old stone walls crisscrossing all through the forest like the ruins of an undersea Atlantis.

We weren't supervised. The men were busy, and the women were at home and busy too. We'd ride over to the lake in a pack on hot days and find some unoccupied beach, throw down our bikes and jump in in our clothes, and if the summer people came out we'd hello them and leave soon after. That was the unofficial rule, we were welcome on the private property around the lake, but not *that* welcome unless there were kids in the house that came out and joined us. Then we might stay all day if they wanted to keep playing with us. We'd be laughing all the time amongst ourselves, we'd be as loud as we could be, the trees and the open water ringing with our noise, no reason to be quiet out here. But even then we knew the score. We were extinct. It might take another fifty years to wash the bones, but it was already God's truth we weren't needed anymore. Nobody depended on us to do what the generations before us had done, they—our parents, like those before them—could do it for themselves until the day they died. And then the life that's been the life of this place for hundreds of years will be over. We're idle hands and extra mouths to feed when idle hands and extra mouths might not cost much, but it hurts to see young strong men and women without much to do or to look forward to. Even if we weren't conscious of it, and certainly didn't have words for it as I do now, we still knew everything, the whole picture, maybe we kids knew it better than the adults did in some ways. I can't even tell you what it was like but it's what it *was*, and it's who we were too.

I've known every good thing there is to know. I'm thirty-one now, an age that's neither old nor young. I can't say I've been much of a father, but I'm here and all three kids, Marie and Ed and little Harold, well, they know it. And Jennie knows it. I'm here and I'm their dad and her former husband, and I'll do anything for them or for her that they ask me to. If I can. I'll do it whatever it is.

~

The world was slowly slipping away is how I'd put it. I saw it all go. We had 100 acres, a good-sized farm by the standards of this state, if only we had had the hands to work it. You look back far enough maybe we had 300 acres. I don't know. We could always farm some, sell off timber or sell some land if ever we needed to. It was a comfortable enough, secure life up until my father's father's time, even in my father's time too. I saw it all. My childhood wasn't filled with troubles. My parents didn't fight. They were expectant, more willing, more likeable actually than their surroundings were. And all the changes that had been in the making for decades leading up to me actually began taking place in my time and I saw it all: the woods creeping back into the fields, first with fast-growing weed trees, the silver maple and green ash, then the hardier, better, more deeply rooted, deep-drinking tall-growing ones, elm and oak, beech, white pine and sugar maple—and we stepped back and let them because we didn't really need fields now as we once had, didn't feel them inside us in the same way as we had before either.

I saw it, just like when you see a crime happen before your eyes and it isn't like it is on television. I've seen men kick their dogs, I've seen the look men give their women that means they will hurt them physically later when there aren't any people around and it can be their little secret. And it's a trick of time that tells you something happening now is taking place also in the future, that it's complete and full, a measure of time that begins now and goes on forever. I saw the long rows of yellow-tasseled New Hampshire corn, and also the hillsides where a hundred apple trees paraded in neat rows, twenty feet apart, the individual trees like cripples, or at least laborers, but the rows stately like a procession in a church but gay and joyous in a way no church procession ever was or could be. I saw those things dry up and go away. There were fewer corn fields and apple orchards at first. Fewer trees tapped for maple syrup. My parents began to sell off parcels of land we didn't need or want when they could. Then there were no orchards along the road at all. Just, here and there, in a crease of land, two or three gnarled old trees hanging on. The fields are still shapely, still have their character, not flat but rolling, with stands of different kinds of trees dotting them here and there for different reasons, usually because they're around a boulder too large to move, a few trees that grow tall and strong in the open sunlight and protected from the tractor by that boulder. But the fields, pretty as they may be, serve no purpose now, have no reason to be here except to rest troubled eyes. This isn't to complain, I never liked doing fieldwork, but what a difference from how it used to be! And I saw it both ways, before and after. And I'm from here, so the shock and wonder of it is as close as you'll get to a dictionary definition of myself. In me is the gracious and giving land as it was before, and in me along with the rest of my generation is a place uprooted and cast aside.

You think you know what is a man. You say we're selfish, only care about ourselves. I can tell you for certain that isn't how it is.

If we only wanted to have things our way, then how is it that when you give us everything just how we like it, we aren't happy? Wouldn't we be benevolent towards you, towards everyone, if getting the things we want was what made us tick?

I've never met a selfish man. I've known men, and boys too, that like to kill things, men that are never satisfied no matter what they get. Anyway, men around here don't get much.

First of all, if you are a woman and you are scared of your man, even a little, then how can you be close to him, or a comfort to him? Even a dog will love a man or a woman no matter how it's treated because a dog doesn't care about itself in that way. But a woman does care how she's treated no matter what she says, and if she fears a man she can never truly love that man. Which is why every single man alive dreams of a fearless woman, and also why the thing that drives men, the one thing, is measuring up.

I was a man even before I was fully grown. I never thought my brother was. So when he came back to us hurt, it made a kind of sense to me. It achieved certain unspoken goals. Now, with his disability, he'd never have to work. He could stay longer with ma. He could take his time and reflect, as he had always enjoyed doing. He didn't seem to be in much physical pain, more discomfort and not being able to do some things. I think there must always be that sense of destiny when something like that happens, the way the whole past all suddenly seems to be leading up to the injury or the death that stops time.

Our farm was on the road into the town of Ashland, but nearer to the lake. So growing up we did get to know some of the families that came up from Boston, Massachussetts, or Providence, Rhode Island, with their families for their summer vacations, or to go winter skiing, buying lakeside cabins or houses in the woods like the Richardson place, places that got sold sometimes because a couple was childless, and then one dies, and the other doesn't want the trouble of a big house. It was a gradual invasion, and we were curious about those kids, and they were curious about us.

Just past our property was the border among four different towns, New Hampton, Ashland, Center Harbor and Meredith, which meant that when it came time to start school, there were four different yellow school buses going in four different directions, and I was the only one I knew going to the Ashland school, and of the four towns Ashland was I guess the dirtiest, because of the mills, so no one really wanted to go there, but in my family school wasn't ever something welcoming, or even a chance for improvement. It was just something you did because you had to by law, something that was understood to be an unfriendly and useless obligation, time wasted that now can't be spent more fruitfully as it could have been in any one of a number of other ways, whether working or even just doing nothing, but in the right way. That was how we looked at it. School has never done much for our family, or mattered much or changed our direction at all. So when my brother and I started going to school in Ashland, we did it without a very good attitude or any of my childhood friends. And even for my brother, it was the same I think, a waste. Harder for him, since he was the more accomodating one.

Ma doted on me. I was her second son, the last one. She never really saw us as almost-twins, but as her older son and her baby. Ma was large, a comfort to us that way, physically, she moved purposefully and I buried my head in her skirts, in her good smell, since I was shy too. She'd look out and make it all safe for me.

Later on she worked at the Five and Dollar in town, and people liked her there, and she'd come home always with gladness about where she'd been and what she was coming home to. Our dogs were about my best friends, and sometimes there were pups that we'd give away to anyone that wanted them. I was always a good-looking kid with a fierce look. I think I scared ma a little. She didn't know what was in me, and I didn't either. I never thought of myself in terms of smart or not smart, since nothing around us required us to be smart or not smart. We were already smarter than we needed to be. No one talked much. We weren't waiting for anything, and nothing was waiting for us.

You look at the Civil War monument in the town center, and the veterans plaque by the VFW. They tell you a lot about this town. Almost every family sent at least one child off to war, because it was a job. And the boys wouldn't always come back or when they did some came back smashed up, sorely injured, and that was how it was because then you had veteran's disability benefits. My brother went off to Vietnam as a marine, and came back decorated and injured and quiet mostly, receiving his monthly check. Getting that check without having to work for it was good.

We're all born to die, and when I think about how we were as kids I'm almost ashamed how happy we were. And if I'm alive today, and if I'm looking forward to being alive again tomorrow, it's not because of Ma's open-hearted generosity, but because of my father's ways and of how he did his best to prepare us. You could even say her kindnesses were false promises, and his beatings warnings of the dangers that lay just ahead.

I love Jennie. I truly do. But I don't think she has done right by me. I am troubled by her. I wish I had fallen in love with a different girl now. You'll ask what has she done to me? I'll tell you some of the things. She was always restless, not selfish, but restless. A woman thinks she is in love with you because her body is in love with your body. She is so heady and proud and satisfied in herself because she believes at first that she will never betray you. That's her strength and her superiority. She is not even in the least bit tempted. She wants no other man. She only wants you, and that's for her whole life to come, until death descends in one form or another and throws its blanket over you both. So she knows she's better than you. And she is proud of that fact. But she doesn't give you her mind. She has her secrets, that's none of your business. She thinks she knows what men want and that all a woman has to do is give a man what he wants and that's that. Then he leaves her be and is satisfied. But doesn't she see, too, that that leaves a man unsatisfied and alone? No, for some reason, maybe because it isn't convenient, she does not see that.

A woman loves her kids more than she loves you. That's another thing that's unhealthy. The best way would be that a man and a woman love each other most, and with that love make their kids, and teach their kids to see that love and to learn from it, a love based on mutual trust, all-in. A child may want more, but this whole idea of giving someone what they want and thinking that's enough, it's not right. It's demeaning, of the people, and of the love itself that should be there between them.

Jennie did not know that I would never cheat on her. She held the conventional wisdom that all men cheat or want to, and that makes women set their expectations lower, much lower—I don't want to know. He might be. I hope he isn't. How is that okay? She could always trust me, I would never do anything to hurt her, I couldn't have betrayed her even when I'm angry at her, it could never happen. I would die first.

A man believes his woman is not cheating, whether she is or not, and that's blind trust, but one-sided. The woman needs to know the same thing. And that takes a lot of confidence, self-confidence I mean. But how can a woman have that much self-confidence if she spends her life mostly around her children, if she doesn't work, if she is a kind of captive I mean?

Part Four

Jennie (1981)

In February, we rely heavily on the Ashland town library to rescue us. It isn't the books mainly, or even the salt pleasantries of Susan and Jack, the librarians, or that the library is a well appointed house on a hill, and cozier inside than our drafty place. Well, it's all these things really. A public place that welcomes us. On certain afternoons, when there is no peace for me anywhere, I grab the kids and bring them here like we were escaping some primordial terror.

Main street is coated in a hoarfrost. Things are running normally. The shops are open and the Christmas decorations still adorn the high places, swinging across the sky from lamppost to lamppost. But the cold leaves the taste of the morgue on everything, a deadness. Inside, we linger at certain shelves, always the same ones, pretending the cold outside isn't still grabbing at our throats.

Every summer erases the memory of the last winter because in every summer day there is an eternity, the promise that it will last forever. Every winter then comes as a shock, like it were the first one, a fall from grace, a punishment from God for trespasses against Him. I can't remember what winter was like last year. But this year, 1981, the harsh, relentless, stony cold has just burrowed into us like a plague. At school, the children tell me, the radiators shake with the effort and there is frost covering the windows on the inside.

Later, at home, we look over the books we've borrowed. Sometimes there is no meaning in them and I don't remember choosing them. They are like blocks of ice, and I set them aside. But on better days, I open one, and read a few pages, and for a little while I am transported from myself to another plane that is not a place but just a welcoming quietness. And I read to the children, which they love. They follow the story with a concentration and a willingness that shows me the power in them, especially since it travels from one to another in likeness, the same furrowed brow of concentration, from Marie to Ed, and then imitated by Harold even sometimes, the three of them in a clump like teddy bears on the bed, all arms and legs and wide-eyed.

There are warm spells when sometimes a colorless rain falls on our frozen world. Out at Ellie's place, slush forms over the lake ice, and big ice slabs form in the brook in shapes that remind me of giant fish bones. We walk in the rain, holding hands and carrying walking sticks to minimize the chances of falling on the sodden ice. I wear a yellow raincoat and matching yellow hat, and three layers of sweaters, all my hair gathered under the silver and yellow hood like some kind of ageless jalopy, a traveler let's say from outer space would be a kind way to put it. And when we go inside and gather around the fireplace, all my layers let off steam, and when I strip and throw them down in a pile I'm only wearing long underwear and everyone laughs at me which is nice. What's naked though isn't what I'm wearing or not wearing, but just how tired I am, no jokes in me, no stories either, just some nameless burden I am carrying and how it separates me from all these people that I love so much.

There is no such thing as suicide. Something I've learned in the same way as a child learns there is no Santa Claus. There's only life. You dive into it. Every day you're jumping off rooftops and diving under moving trains, you're swallowing swords and walking on coals. That's just living.

People don't know what happens after. Any more than they know what comes before. Shit, people don't know what happens *during* either, not much anyway!

I learned how to love a man through loving Andy. There was never anyone else, not even on television or in my dreams. Just him. My words, my words, my niece says. But I don't have words in the way she does. The first time I saw him was on the wall, it must have been in September, I was thirteen and he was twenty-one. We were made for each other, and that's just how it was. Once we started going out we'd drive around in his truck, not saying much.

But here's the thing. I'm wild. I mean, in my innermost being I am. I knew he loved me. I did too. That gave me wings. I tasted real freedom. There was nothing I needed or could have dreamed having that Andy wouldn't have given me. So it was always dangerous for us to be together. I had no fear with him. If I had asked him to rob a bank he'd have asked me which one. If I'd asked him to drive us off a cliff, same thing.

In a situation like ours, a true-love situation, the body opens up and expresses it. I'm not saying children can't be born of rape or what-have-you. But when two people love each other, like we do, then when you make a baby together it is a union of souls, an expression of love. You feel it so. And that's how it was with us. Like, I mean, when people do drugs who like doing drugs, this is the feeling they are willing to die for, just the rightness of it, aiming for that at almost any cost, and that was how it was and is between him and me, only without the drugs. Andy is my other half, I am his. And that is forever and always. And so, when I have given birth to our children, it is inexplicable, something much bigger than me or than him, a miracle really. I hate to sound like this, so brain-washed. But I just want to say these things, about the rightness of everything, to give you some perspective on the things that happened that you would say cancel these things out. I want you to know, they don't. Only, I paid a price, and we all do, the only price worth paying, the heaviest price. If you want happiness, I swear to you on the God I do sometimes believe in—if you want happiness, go for it, but accept that it may come at the price of unbearable misery. I don't know why, and I'm not saying it always has to be that way.

About dying, we're the only animals I've ever seen that make such a show of it. A dog goes off quietly into a corner. A wolf separates itself from the pack. Of course, it's because we find life so sweet, so tantalizing, that we have trouble accepting we will lose it. But that's only part of it. It's also because we find the sweetness of life so often out of our reach. We are so rarely satisfied. What it most definitely isn't is that we know something the other animals don't. Whoever said we're the most intelligent animal? I'm sure that isn't true. Only a stupid animal would think they're the most intelligent, there's no wisdom in thinking so.

And anyway, why would we be? Because we manipulate all the other ones, domesticate them, turn forests into fields and metals into weapons and tools? We still cannot even control our own selves or find safety. Most animals, I could even say *all* other animals know better than us how to thrive, how to be who or what they are. These are worthier achievements than having power over others.

So we do what we can to be happy, and whether we admit to it or not, we are willing, each of us, secretly, to accept that it's never ever free, that you always pay the most for the things that matter most to you. And that's love too, no exceptions. Every living thing knows this. The tree that rises towards the sun and surmounts the canopy falls the loudest every time.

I want to say something else, about what I was talking about earlier, about love. It's that Andy knows everything. Whatever happens, he knows I love him, that we love each other, and the children, Marie and Ed and even Harold, I have to believe they all know it too. There's just no way they couldn't.

Ellie was never in perfect alignment when we were growing up because she was always the first line of defense, I the littler child, Ellie caught between our mother and me, me always watching them both, mama giving us all she could, great big hugs, as she prepared to go.

She never said to us, Don't you want me to be happy? But she didn't have to. She was a free woman. Because of her we were missing some of the things we needed, some of the comforts and the certainties. But against that, we just adored her. She was still just a very young woman herself, and if there was anything she feared she didn't show it. She taught us courage and she never had to say a word about being brave. She just was.

Maybe I was always fatalistic. I'm not proud of it. But along with that, I am someone who carries within herself great good will towards those I love the most. I am only just observing this about myself. I don't know why it is, unless it's kind of a marriage of opposites, of hopelessness with a kind of belief in people. Kids understand it viscerally, and always trust me and like me for it. Maybe it's because it's not exactly mature of me to rush headlong into everything the way I do. I don't know. I can observe myself, but I cannot say I understand myself, does anybody?

Suicide is a very cold-sounding term, not even a word really, but rather shorthand for history itself. Once it was thought of as something admirable and altruistic, an honorable action for Romans to initiate as a worthy end to a worthy life. Only with organized religion did it begin to have an ugly smell to it, because it meant taking away from a vengeful God his power over us. If God cannot decide who lives and when death comes, then what power is there vested in God actually? And today, well, the state would also say as much. When a serial killer takes his own life, there is a kind of nonstory ending, as if one moral code were violated and another one asserted that is too dangerous. Don't think I am pretending to know more than I do. I only read one old book. I'm no expert.

To be or not to be? Beautiful. A question. Questions are always beautiful.

It's easy enough to say that no one knows what happens after we die. Just as we don't know what came before we were born. I thought I knew. And I even believed that's what made me special, not just to others, even to my own self. I knew what life was for. It made me who I was. I loved my life, and all the people in it.

People who do away with themselves aren't unhappy souls. Maybe some are, but not most. And it can be the very opposite. Some suicides know a happiness so rare and good inside themselves. I can promise you this. And they hold onto it, tightly and tenderly no matter what, like some leaf trembling where there's no wind. You marvel at the leaf, and then you realize that your hand is shaking. And so they just let go, because pain comes, a pain like childbirth or some other change, something unforeseen, but also because who is to say you have to always hold on, hold on for dear life? Sometimes you can say, I have lived so much already, or my time isn't always now. Or that you have survived and again survived, and thrived, and fought and won, but you cannot survive and win every time, no one can.

My sister Ellie and me, three years separate us, but it isn't as if she's always the older one and me the younger one. Yes, sometimes she bends in the wind so that I might stand perfectly straight beside her. Sometimes she waits so that I can press on past her. She does not speak first to silence me. It is, well, it has always been—I don't know how—that Ellie looks up to me. She says, You amaze me. And maybe I do. I don't have to do anything. I don't even know what it is that I do. Just being alive means that she isn't alone, that there are always at least two of us. And that's true for us both, needless to say. And it was our consolation, but also the hardship we grew up with, since we were always thankfully two, but never three with our mother as we would have wished for more than anything. She was gone, and we were two. And so it was more like stars aligned than like a family. And saying I was everything to Ellie isn't saying too much or even enough. I was her happiness and she was always mine too. But in a completely different way. I was strong and she wrapped around me like a vine, protecting me from harm of course, but also drinking me in and living through me and finding some happiness, though not her very own, in just me being here too, filling the space and the time that we had here together, two entwined young souls.

So miracles is a word I like well enough, a pagan-sounding word. A lot of the time people want to say there's no such thing. But the real problem with miracles isn't that they don't exist. It's almost the very opposite. That there are multitudes of them, in us and all around us, every moment. In fact most things are best understood as miracles. The lives we made, Carolyn's, then Marie's, then Ed's and last my Harold's. Out of emptiness. Ellie and me are our own miracles, needless to say, no brain or body could have made us, we just are. And in this place every life that defies winter and hate, all the beauty without a name. Every second of every minute and every minute of every day. The taste of water, and the taste too of the air in our lungs, the breathing in and the breathing out. Miracles that grow out of our need to make miracles. We don't have to prove them or even announce them. It is fine that we keep them hidden, even from ourselves. But let our eyes shine with pride nonetheless for all that we have done, even though we were only two helpless teenage girls.

~

Once you have loved someone and been loved in return, it is a place and a way of being you can return to, there inside you, unchanging.

I think of it as a blessing, it means you have a past.

So when this happened, I didn't see it coming at all. I mean, I was looking, hoping. But I wasn't ready to give up Andy. I had divorced him, but at the same time I was still holding on to him, even if away from myself. Divorcing Andy was easy by comparison with what was happening now, putting a new man in his place, someone I hardly knew at first in place of someone who was my second self.

After I ended things with Andy, he was still everywhere in my consciousness. I had distanced myself, but not actually rid myself of him. That would have been impossible to do. Marie and Ed and Harold all love him, and so do I so long as I don't have to live under him as man and wife. Our marriage was the nail in the coffin. I'm so glad we went through with it because it meant I could finally then get free of the man I loved. But what I didn't realize at all was that in the end nothing matters until you decide what you're willing to let go. I wasn't ready.

Edith (1981)

I don't believe in luck. It goes against my religious faith, every bit as much as suicide does. And yet plain luck does seem to be such a force in the world. I wish I could stare it down and make it go away and believe that only God decides. But I cannot, since so much that happens seems to be accountable to plain, dumb luck.

I don't think Gordon cares one way or the other about practicing our religion. His God doesn't reside in our church. He—Gordon I mean, my husband Gordon, not God, for God's sake—has the great gift of seeing some bounteousness almost everywhere he turns—in people, in crafts and art, in how the weather changes violently and returns gently. Nature's bounty. He has no quarrel with any god, but no need of one either. There is no despondency in him, ever—that isn't one of the songs in his repertoire—or if it is he hides it from me. He is the kind of bird you hear, issuing forth from the underbrush, delighted with itself, wipperwee-wipperwoo, a song that is as much waiting quietly and listening as it is making sound. My God, I love the man I married, the father of my children. He doesn't deem it necessary to linger in shadowy places. Too much that needs doing, every waking moment already accounted for. And anyway, he must offset me, I do understand that. I am morose much of the day. I lean on my God to shed some constant light on things for me. And if there is transparency and meaning in my watercolor paintings, it is because I let myself be directed by God's hand, none of it is of my own making. My happiness is merely to let God see through me things as they are, beautiful and serenely dying and being born.

But I have so many questions. *Why* questions, the hardest kind. I am as unlike Gordon in this as a fig is from a stone. And these questions I have, I cannot let them go unanswered. They may not be of life and death, but to me they are exactly that, and I'm full, full to brimming over with them. I hardly ever encounter obstacles in the shallows. I can steer myself there. But in deeper waters, what is one to do but suffer and despair? I live with my despair every moment, along with my questions—almost every single waking moment. I do not wish to be shrill, or strident. I am mostly silent in my cares. But they surround me and enter me like demons.

There is a reason why we organize humanity in terms of male and female. And it isn't a good reason, I can tell you. It is to sustain a fallacy—and to hide a truth. The fallacy is that we are all mostly the same. Of two genders, but even so, mostly the same. The truth is the opposite of this: there are almost as many species and genders of humans as there are individual people. We share words, thoughts, aspirations, fears, a love of the beautiful, desire. We comfort ourselves with this small vocabulary of qualities, thinking we are all alike. Binary. Male and female, thrusters and thrusted into, war maker, life giver, etc. Harmonious. Comprehensible.

But it isn't even half true. There are greater differences between us than common ground, disparities far beyond what we would ever wish to imagine. There is little consensus, even as to what is good and what is bad, or whether anything can truly be called good or bad. I don't mean to say we are mad. That too would only be a gross simplification. I mean to say only that we construct our harmonious paintings and friendships, marriages and books, philosophies, marvel at the births, and deaths too, knowing if we were ever going to be honest about it that these are only bits of straw and grains of sand against an onslaught that has no name and us no facility to give it one.

Gordon has always carried himself in a certain way. It's what originally attracted me. The corridors and rooms and porches at the mountain asylum were rustic but grand. I remember seeing him across one of the larger rooms, moving towards where I was sitting near the hearth. I can describe him to you exactly as he was—tall but frail, with a birdcage torso, head set back, and a twinkle in the eye. Well, I know now that he felt like an outsider, that he was putting it on, so it was a studied look after all. But let me say that I am enough of an artist to swoon at things moving in the right combination. He conveyed gentleness and manliness and I will say that after a half-century and more living with him, the message that was emanating from him on that first sighting, well, it has not failed to stir in me a feeling of happiness, and he himself, the man I married, has not failed me either. He has been stalwart. God has failed me, and I have failed God. Many, *many* times. But Gordon hasn't failed me yet, not once. It is eerie. I believe I have some power over him, not one I control or even wish to have. But Gordon believes in me—me, the eternal doubter. How ironic. Call it love. But it's a mean business. I'd rather, honestly, that he were more free and loved me anyway. No woman wants a slave.

Carolyn (1982)

It is 1982, and I am ten. The first anniversary of the moment they met comes and is mentioned and then is already gone, like a shot. Throughout the coldest months of this second very cold winter together, Jennie and Jacosin are nearly always with us here in the big brown house. I enjoy seeing Jennie enjoying herself. It's in the smallest things she does. Enjoying yourself, I learn now, can be the opposite of watching yourself. It is specially the opposite of watching yourself enjoying yourself. She plays the fool, mama says, and he's her straight man. Jennie talks loudly, while Jacosin reads quietly with a grin on his face. He talks quietly while she listens hard and blurts things out, interrupting him and bringing the grin to his face again. He gets mad at her for not paying attention enough and she loves him like a happy dog, stomping on his toes and licking his face, mussing him up, until the same grin is back on his face. Sometimes they leave Marie, Ed, and Harold with us for hours that can be a little trying. But I've noticed the same thing that's happening to Jennie is also happening to her three children. They aren't watching themselves as much. They are watching *each other* more, which is one of the best ways not to watch yourself as much.

Outside, we bundle up. All you really see of us is the color of the warm coat and hat and the rest is just a blur except for a general sense of height that is the only way to tell us apart. Marie and I sometimes switch coats and *everyone* calls her Carolyn and me Mah-ree and there isn't even anything funny about it.

It's more like whoever's wearing Marie's coat is Marie and whoever's wearing Carolyn's coat is Carolyn. Period. Sometimes Jacosin and Jennie take the four of us with them and we do kid things when whole afternoons fly by and I can tell it isn't even hard or tiring for Jennie and Jacosin to be with us this way. It is being a perfect family, including mama who gets to have her serious hours alone and then to turn on the porch light and welcome us back at the end and that's just as much being with us as if she'd come along to do whatever it was we were doing. The funniest part, even besides the coats, is how this winter the freezing temperatures that can be a hard turn that makes everything awful doesn't bother us much. There is a whirlwind in and around us that is our special season and it is the opposite of the weather. And the best part is how we kids think it is the most normal thing that everyone should get along and everything should go this well.

One night when we're laying in her bed half asleep but not yet warm mama says, in a way I don't like, Jennie is happy but her happiness flows over her like it isn't her own. What's good has happened so suddenly, there hasn't been time for it to change her. She feels it wash over her. I know that feeling, too. Mama isn't talking to me exactly when she says that. She's upset, talking to nobody, shaking a little with the cold because however many blankets there are over us they haven't warmed us up yet, choosing the words that go with the natural shaking in her bones.

Jacosin comes over by himself after work sometimes too, driving slowly up the driveway, then walking slowly over from his car to wherever we are. Exaggerating the slowness, I guess, of life in the moments when Jennie isn't beside him, like he's making a joke of how painfully slow it is and at the same time he means it: Without Jennie I can't really do more than just get from point A to point B. As if he were conveying to mama and me that idea or something similar. But we all know that we will be happily together as we are now for years and years, forever, and it is that, really, that pleases us kids the most. None of us have ever had anything before that we didn't feel couldn't be taken away at any moment. So Jacosin's slow walk is definitely a joke we can all appreciate and enjoy, since there will never come a time when he's not with Jennie.

The last traces of winter are the brittle stubble in the fields, the occasional last pocket of snow glinting diamonds, the air wet and the sodden ground half drowning, a dripping sponge. The melt comes down off the mountains like driving pistons, every mountain stream and rivulet a rushing river now, a low roar that fills the ear from above and below, from this side and that side. The sun as yet emits only a cold seasonal glare, the days are still short and uncertain. We emerge from the rock-solid ice world of the last winter months, the coldest ones, a little dazed at first, as if only just discovering that the armies of winter have fled without a victory for either side.

After winter, Spring 1982 is a different kind of story. We celebrate my birthday and then Marie's with a gladness that is quiet and full, patient and long-rested, with a childishness that, for us, seems a little adult-like, and mama and Jennie looking finally like a winning team after all the years when they were always losing. The longer days of April, and the gentle rains. Green shoots that thrust out of the ground with authority. The careening finches and swallows, buntings, sparrows, drawing lines of joy in synchronous statements of fact and hesitant questions, the lumbering crows notwithstanding. Every branch of every tree sending out leaves in so many different varieties of green and endless repetitions of size and shape.

Jacosin has decided to dedicate himself to patching our shingle roof. Our long ladder spends the lengthening days and shorter nights leaning against the house on one side or the other, and a couple of times a week Jacosin is up there, wearing his leather apron, working on one area or another. Instead of barreling in like a conqueror, he has entered our world like a field mouse. And in this early start to his second summer with Jennie, the first with us, he is somehow already part of us, tapping here and there on the outer shell, repairing here, circling there.

It's summer, and the lake is waiting, strumming its fingers. Most mornings I'm up early and soon walking down the path, the sun still in the upper branches, my black plastic tackle box in my left hand and my slender casting rod in my right. A shiny lure of silver or gold, what we fisherwomen call a spoon, with a treble hook dangling from it, bounces from the tip like a tiny lantern, my little light nesting in the illumination of the already limitless day

I stride with big steps down to the water's edge, strap on my orange life preserver damp with morning dew, step into my broken-down plexiglass, so-called glass-bottom, scratched-everywhere boat, and set out. From our shore I don't see the two islands yet—Thunder Island, smaller and nearer, then Boulder Island, larger and further out—that together form the waist of the hourglass. The further out I go, the more the far distance comes to meet me. As I row I crane my neck around, and at some point I pass an invisible border line. From the inward gaze of our cove, I see a vastness now—the pine-crested mountains rising above me for miles. There is the illusion of a soft seam between the clean line of the mountains and the great expanse of changing sky. And below them, right in front of me, the seven-story-high white pines rise up from the first island, a water-colored bit of land so separate and distant from other land masses that it seems itself to be a few steps up some invisible ladder, blurring together land, water, sky. The silhouette I make, seated in my low, rectangular, peculiar, see-through rowboat is known to our neighbors. Solitary child sitting alert and hesitant in her doubtful little boat. Something of the gremlin or ghoul about me, bent over and hardly moving while the boat drifts along.

It will come to haunt me when I learn that my father and I have shared not only these surroundings but also the glass bottom boat. Is the cat's cradle I make going back and forth across the lake identical to one he made, or totally different? I'll never know whether a leg or a hand or a cast or a catch or a moment of rest is truly mine or was his first and is mine only in the reinvention, an echo, an inheritance.

I push off, float away, and wait for myself—the way you wait for a friend at a bus stop, intently, all but shutting down until the friend arrives, when—but only then—the machinery of time, including your heartbeat, returns to the usual hum of activity. But there have been delays apparently. Waiting might be fruitless. The held breath is kept in. The hours come and go. I cast under trees and rafts or out into the open water. You never know where the fish might be. I go from one end of the lake to the other and back again. And sometimes I bring home a good size pickerel or bass, with the hours of sunlight and wind mixed in with my sweat. And each day the near mountains speak to me. But I never catch what I am casting for, and most often I return with no fish at all. I trudge back up to the house from the lake in the early afternoon, refreshed for having had the time alone, but also with the unanswered question still lingering, the thing I want badly to happen, the self-discovery, eluding me again. I've been tested by the hours alone, though. And sometimes my feet feel unaccustomed to the solid ground. I am filled with the conviction that we are saved, and have no need of anything that we don't already have in us, that my certainty is enough, is more than enough.

Sometimes I am met on my return from the lake by the empty house in the still and silent afternoon. On other days, a half-dozen or more visitors are here talking, reading, or playing, adults and kids together. Jennie's boyfriend Jack, our great discovery still, now one and a half years in, already our crown prince and our pied piper—I can always find the other children by going where Jack is, planing down a door on the porch or on his back under the car, telling his jokes and stories. Jennie so happy with him—the proof that she acts the same as before, takes time for her kids and for me even though she's in love.

Since we're happy here now, obviously so, old friends of Jennie's and mama's come out to see us more often now than before. It isn't unusual for there to be fifteen or more of us, people arriving at the house stepping from their cars with big smiles, casting their eyes upward into brightness and laughing out loud. Even with Jack anointed, this is still a woman's and child's world at a time when that's rare. And for mama and me it is always a relief more than it is an intrusion to have the house full. When there's no one here, although we claim to adore the peace and quiet, the nights are long and even the days are long for us. When there are people around, mama finds her wistful enthusiasm again, sure and uncertain in the way she has, nothing if not charming. Having a crowd around brings something out in her that I don't get to see that often, someone others see but that she doesn't bring out when it's just the two of us. I find somewhere to sit on the porch and have my lunch alone, slowly reentering the peopled world. Already a part of me is considering tomorrow morning's solitary fishing expedition. I am trying to learn how not to get lost in other people. I've already decided that when you strip away everything that has ever happened, there remains an essence, a way of walking with time, like a wheel with no friction that rolls on endlessly, when the thread passing through us from the solid ground beneath to the sky above is unbroken. Between mama and me there are always channels of communication and understanding that no words can describe. Around us, brightness falls in torrents. The fields are buoyant.

The land and the lake sway into and away from each other. On summer weekends, it can be like a county fair here. There's a constant hum of voices, some hushed and others loud. People squeeze in around the picnic table like birds on a wire. Mama and me are alone together no matter how many others are here with us. She sits on the porch knitting a sweater. I read near her, the two of us in a state of constant awareness of each other.

It is 1983. I am eleven now. As summer approaches, Jack's project is to paint the house. Sometimes we bring out deck chairs from the garage and sit there in a cluster to watch him. The gradual changing of the dull brown into a lustrous rich brown affects us. Jennie and Jacosin have finally started to plan their future together. And though they don't exactly argue, I can see it's not going well, as if in trying to plan a future together they really have gone too far. Jennie and Andy's divorce has finally come through. People come around more, to mill about and talk with us, and to watch Jack work. And even though mama would say she couldn't care less what our neighbors think, these are just the kinds of things that matter most to her.

It's 1984. Jack is getting us to read more, sometimes altogether in a group. The two twelve year olds, Mah-ree and me, turn the pages and are the designated leaders. We read aloud, bring the words into the room. As soon as we say each one out loud, it rushes back into the book. You never own them. You only ever borrow them. And they don't so much change you but words do change other words. Every word's meaning can expand so much depending on what other words surround it, and so you see that. They are colored by their surroundings, even as we are. Except time operates differently for them than for us. And yet, thinking about how I can read a story that's old in a book, just as another person might read it a hundred years ago or a hundred years into the future, I can't help thinking we aren't changed by the passage of time any more than words are. Just a suspicion I have, despite appearances.

And then, something else, a small thing. Do we read a book, or does a book read us? If you think about it, you enter a book to learn something about yourself that you didn't know. No one is defined by what we already know about ourselves, such a small and limited repository. You read a story about people and places that are completely foreign, and learn that that too is within the boundaries and the multiplicity of who you are. You read a murder mystery and find, not a victim, but a murderer in you. A book is just ink on paper and board. When you start to read, it enters you and not the other way around. This matters because in times when we have lost our way, as happens to everyone, a book reading us can mean we do exist after all, not in ourselves if we are going to be honest about it, but in books.

Here are the different reading styles in our house: Mama's is the prettiest, Jennie's the loudest, Jacosin's the sweetest-growliest, Marie's and mine the most expressive. The little boys enjoy the complications of all the different ways we have to read a book. I have to be very honest with you: I don't think any of us loves books though, only each other.

It only lasts three years, the good life. Then comes the summer of 1984. We have so much now to lose! No wonder we were unwilling in the past to go this far.

We still see Andy sometimes. The first time he comes by when Jacosin is here, Andy gets out of his car and starts to walk over to where Mah-ree and Ed and Harold and I are. Then Jack comes around the house and they both stop and it's just the two of them standing there for a little while.

Not only are we more comfortable with Jacosin than with Andy, we're better without Andy, period, I have to admit. I don't understand how or why that is. We all love Andy so much. But the less he's here, the happier we are. Almost as if his absence were someone new we really like.

Once I come into the house and there's Jennie looking at herself in the stained mirror above the open fireplace. All the other children are outside with mama. It is a bright summer day, a Saturday in August. Inside, it's cool and there is the tin sheen that the house has, how it keeps the daylight out. Instead of going up to her or announcing myself, I stay where I am and watch her. What I see is something I've never seen before in anyone, a look on her face that says she's studying herself in the way a scientist would study a research subject, a monkey or a dog that's been cut open, so you can see it's organs pumping, knowing it will die as a result of this experiment, but it's all in the larger interests of progress. There is something triumphant in her look. As if she had gone mad, but was doing a good job hiding the fact, not letting us see that this is how she really is. Jennie, so luminous, under the cold stare of this other person I don't recognize. I go back outside, embarrassed, leaving her to her sadness. I feel pushed, as if by a gust of wind. And Jennie herself never notices me, so absorbed is she in her investigations.

It is the summer of 1984 and mama and I are walking together down the path from the house to the lake. Our eyes are downcast, scanning the ground we walk along for branches, wasps, snakes. We have nothing to say, which is unusual for us on our walks. There is a steady wind that must be a force to reckon with in the treetops because in our ears the sound that falls from there is tremendous and we are a little shocked by how loud it is: a million leaves spinning on their stems sounding as I imagine stones under the sea do when rolled by the tide.

I know the sound, it is the end approaching, not near yet, but coming, and what really scares me is how familiar it is to me, as if I were born hearing it. The hour isn't early or late, mid-morning say, or early afternoon. There is a weekday quiet in the air. It might be a Thursday. Jennie and the kids haven't been here for a week or more. This stirs us up and silences us. Where is she?

Stepping along the broad path that, like poured sugar, the field empties into, and in turn that itself empties through the marsh, onto the beach and then into the lake, we are walking in the old way, terribly close, mother and daughter of one body. But the old way has ended. I don't know how we both know that, but we do. Instead of the comfort of walking side by side, touching, there is a new awkwardness between us.

In our summer garden, the tomatoes and lettuces, cucumbers, zucchini, and green peppers are prospering. The path is thick with insects. We've seen a lot of hummingbirds this year, and Monarch butterflies, along with the bees and wasps and mosquitoes and horseflies, the dragonflies in a range of sizes and colors, and all the rest, the ones that bite and the ones that don't. The sun has been gentle and gracious and the rainy days few and far between. In every arc of every day, the same sounds and stirrings. Holding on, holding on. The first stirrings of the end of summer are still far off. Not yet the occasional first solitary tree blazing orange and yellow. Not yet the scented breath of the lilies we transplant from the forest floor or the white phlox. It is June still, or early July, the time when summer is still never-ending, and a long look back or a long look ahead show nothing but more summer. A quiet mid-summer day. I mean, pretty much perfect. But even though I want to say nothing could ever come between mama on me on such a perfect day, it isn't nothing. There's a chain reaction starting, and now quickening. We both feel it, at the same time as it would be impossible to say what it is. So we just catch each other's eyes, share a look, and keep moving.

Part Five

Carolyn (1984)

That day, Jennie comes over with the kids in the afternoon and after they settle in she says to Marie and me, A walk girls? On her face she wears a peaceful smile. She looks beautiful and untroubled, fully in the moment, not wanting anything she doesn't have already, nothing more than to walk on the land with her niece and her daughter.

Everything we have here is so complete that we are easily persuaded it will be with us permanently even though it turns out to be ours only for a little while—three years. I won't ever let mama or Marie or anyone suggest it wasn't real. For a time we have enough, more than enough. Mama and I can go walking, and at the end when it comes time to stop and turn around, and we return along the same path, it's to find things we haven't noticed before. All the old places dawn in this way over and over. The things that never change are never the same way twice either. We know ourselves. And whatever emptiness there is we can always fill with the smell of water and stone, the touch of green and gray, and the way the ground pushes back against our feet. I will remember too the raggedness and a deep unsteadiness at the edges, a fluttering. But it isn't something that frightens us. It is just the natural border between things.

One thing I'll never say is that she wasn't happy. I mean, she was her own person, happy when she was, and at other times not, like most people. What was different about her that made her take her own life, with so much love around her, with her life ahead of her, and not wanting to hurt anyone, is a question without an answer that I can provide.

Mama spreads her sister's ashes on a windless and overcast Monday morning in late September. Whatever was here before has proved temporary. Whatever has replaced it will be here forever. Mama has us gather in the middle of the front field where Jennie concocted her wild iris garden out of plants she found on the forest floor on her walks, and they thrive in the open field and return each year more plentiful than the year before. The flowers bloomed at the end of the summer, but the faded blossoms are like parchment and the stalks are still bright green. Mama pours Jennie's cup of white ash and bone bits over them, and then she bends over and presses the ash into the soil so it won't just blow away.

Andy brings Marie and Ed and Harold and his new girl is with them. He and the kids walk over to where mama and I are and wraps us in his arms. Jacosin nods to him and they also embrace. Gordon and Edith are here. There is a rare kindly smile on Edith's face, with her knowledge of death and how not to be afraid of it. And on Gordon's face, contrastingly, a rare grimace. My father's mother is here, weeping because to her what Jennie dies from is a general murderousness that she is part of and it all could have been so different. Other women Jennie's age that I don't know, some with children, come to mourn one of their comrades fallen in battle. The great aunts come, their faces as pale as the silver bracelets up and down their arms.

Mrs. Mills stands facing us and speaks. Nothing important except when she says Jennie's name and then each of the children's names. I keep Jacosin as close as I can. His sadness is half-sweet and somehow speaks to mine. He's returning to his life as it was before he met Jennie, one he likes well enough. And now it is fuller. Jennie's ghostly presence will be his companion forever, like a book he's re-reading, understanding a little more now than before each time he opens it, closing it after a sentence or two, picking it up again in a few days or a few months, the water always flowing whether he dips his hand in or not.

Jacosin is standing on the top granite step outside the town library in the center of Ashland on the Tuesday morning right after our homegrown Monday morning service for Jennie, and rests there for a moment before starting his day, amazed by everything. The doorknob in his hand is the same one he's turned a few thousand times over the last five years without once ever really looking at it. But he looks now. At the door knob, and then the door, and then raises his head to take in the whole house that has stood here some two hundred and forty years, pretty much the same as now. He peers again at the knob and bits of old paint imbedded in it. And wonders if the coppery green were once a primary color, and if the dark brown had once been fire-engine red? He considers also how every adult and child that climbs these stairs and turns the knob polishes it and smoothes it.

Once inside, he finds his usual seat, his back to the picture window overlooking the little park across Main Street and the patch of river beyond, and doesn't feel at all disappointed to have made a simple and unremarkable life for himself here. He thinks to himself on such a bright and glorious morning as this one that the dead exist somewhere, and that wherever they are they must be a little tired of our obsession with them. He feels relieved, for Jennie's sake. He sees now that she carried on her shoulders a terrible weight of happiness and unhappiness, too much for one person to carry. He sees too that nothing is ever destroyed without leaving some trace. Sometimes, in the coming days and months, and even years, sitting at his desk here in the library, Jack plays the chess game of what if, but not mostly.

Part Six

Carolyn (1984)

Cotton Candy Heads. Toothbrushes. *Pinus strobus.* White pine. Our clown sentinels. Built like fortresses, rising above the canopy formed by the other trees. Drawing the fire of lightening flashes during storms. Solitary friendly monsters, ugly and gross featured, strong and beautiful, the lion kings of this woodland realm. Ships' masts. Once or twice a year, a forester will drive up and offer to thin out the forest for us by taking down our white pine. They offer good money, and present this as healthy forest management, which maybe it is. But we are as protective of our friends as if they were our children and no more likely to sell them. We listen, warily, and look at these men standing there, kicking the dirt and looking at their boots and then at us. We thank them and look them straight in the eye, mama and me ourselves honorary *pinus strobuses.* We offer the men coffee, and tell them we will think about it, but our meaning couldn't be clearer and they understand us perfectly.

Perverse sorcery to build something with a ship's mast and pine needles in clusters woven together like sails and then give it earthbound roots, and yet here they are all around us, the work of the ages. Unruly creatures of real power and wildness, at odds with the natural world as much as they are a part of it. The sharp remnants of dead lower branches sticking out from the trunks like arrows broken off in the bodies of the martyrs—Saint Sebastians Edith calls them—while around the massive trunks on the forest floor their soft beds spread out of pine needles and moss.

It is sometime in August 1984, maybe five weeks after Jennie dies. I'm standing in the large front field halfway down the slope between the house and the woods when I notice a large doe at the forest edge, still some distance from the house but nearer to me, crystallizing in the mid-morning light something I could never put into words, some fact connecting me and everything else, like we were all composed this way and the split second itself were part of the composition, all made out of some porous material as light as air and as strong as iron. I can pick out the features of her face and small muscles flickering on her neck and body. Now that she's entered my world, having embraced the safety of our miserable quietness, she will stay for what seems like hours. I do nothing but watch her for the longest time. We've embarked on a philosophical discussion, she by lowering her long neck to feed on the grass, raising her head from time to time, unrushed, attentive, I by interpreting her slightest movements even as she studies mine. Nothing intrudes upon us, so important to us both is this gift exchange. At some point, keeping her unblinking eyes on me, she folds her legs under herself and sits. I remain standing, awkwardly, my body pointed down the slope, my head turned to the right facing her. I reach over and rub myself along my ribs under my left breast, still almost like a boy's breast. After a while, her jaw working as she thoughtfully chews again the grass she's eaten, she closes her eyes, chewing all the while. I don't move, alternating between an unbearable physical restlessness and a kind of trance that might have lasted as long as three, four, maybe five whole minutes, an eternity if you're standing in a field with your head turned. She opens her eyes again. Then she rises and returns to grazing, her eyes on me, our conversation ongoing.

Julius—my collie-beagle mix—lies sleeping in the middle of the driveway in front of the house, whimpering as she chases squirrels across her dreams, her paws scraping the dirt. I can hear the locked-air sound of a door upstairs shutting, and then of my grandmother, my father's mother, suddenly our frequent guest during these difficult days, exhaling as she lowers herself onto a bed, preparing to rest after staying up through the night with mama again, the noises traveling through the open windows and into my ear like someone whispering just to me. Mama herself I can hear fussing in the kitchen, while on the stove something slow-cooks in a giant pot. I feel intensely the tiny, far-off flame, even though I cannot see it. After making a good show of getting through the morning, mama is faltering now too, soon to find her bed and the only few hours of sleep she'll have before the next sleepless night. The wheels of the day barely turn at all. The wind stirs the curtains in the open windows and the tree-tops. Otherwise, there is a pause of the physical world—not of contentment, not of the fruit hanging heavily on the bough, though this is the warm and gentle month leading into the harvest season. Something else. Time slowing itself down. Not to restore itself, just the reluctant and final end of some part of us now that these are different times.

Finally the doe's scent awakens Julius, she stands stiffly, still half asleep, barking at the sky, torturing herself for failing to protect mama and me from the intrusion, dragging her backside low to the ground, displaying the anguish of her wounded pride. And in the ruckus I miss the moment the doe turns and disappears back into the thick leafed woods, just as I didn't see her step into the field in the first place. I will talk about the visitation for months, hoping desperately that, in some mysterious and unnamable way, the animal from the forest can guide us through the danger we're in to safety.

I feel the species loneliness that has set in. It is the curse of what happened to Jennie, the after effect, like smoke from a cigarette. Exactly as if we still believed in the gods to protect us, and they had abandoned us anyway. The unhurriedness of the doe is a sign to me of hope in the possible return of our protectors, whoever they may be. Only dumb animals can save us from our dumb selves, I decide. We say we're smarter than they are, but we don't really believe that. They encircle us at night, and their attention may be all we have protecting us. I understand, not in words, since mama and I don't talk about it, but still—I understand well enough—what Edith calls our glaring insufficiency, speaking of people in general. It is the plain opposite of what you might expect. Not our inability to muddle through, but our inability not to. This is what we need help with from the wordless world. How to resist the urge always to have to make things better, God help us!

By the end of 1984, Marie, Edward, and Harold have gone to live with a childless couple outside of Philadelphia. Andy showed the great good sense not to try to intervene. The couple, who adopted the three children in the same spirit of forbearance they would have shown to the victims of a natural disaster somewhere far away, an earthquake or some Biblical plague, seem to picture Ashland as far-off in that way because of what happened to Jennie here. To me this is yet another misunderstanding, part of the ruination of understandings and relationships as intricate and delicate as spider webs that were made to endure for our whole lifetimes and now are smashed. We somehow manage to come up with a plan for the children to visit us every June, to suffer the mosquitoes and unearth what they can of their history here, and for two weeks in August, when Andy and Jacosin also come, and the big brown house is again what it always has been, the blessed chaotic crescendo of the symphony we replay over and over, not written by any composer but by some storm of nature that saves us again and again. For a few years, that little plan will be the saving grace in all our lives, island hopping and leap frogging from June to

June and from August to August. But at the same time, it is just too much for mama to be the dog with swollen teats who somehow lays down and nurses us all. And after a few years she will be the teacher who says, I cannot do this again. I don't want to, and I cannot even if I did. And the other kids and I, and Jacosin and Andy too, will stand back when that happens and nod our heads in approval, because we see she is standing up for herself and this means there is hope for us all still, not just an afterlife but an embrace in the here and now, transmuting the catastrophe of what happened to Jennie and thus to Marie and Ed and Harold and mama and me and Andy and Jacosin too, into something else altogether, the love and force of Jennie returning to us in its life-giving shape, and through mama first of all.

I do not have the words yet, but I am preparing the raised beds where later my garden will be. And not just me. Even before we are done mourning, we have begun to reconstitute and reclaim, in their fineness and fragility, some of the mysteries that will emerge later. And sometimes I look at mama in shock and amazement for the resemblance between her and her sister that I see now and never noticed when Jennie was alive. Edward will emerge after Jennie's death as the predator among us, doing terrible things—assassinating bull frogs and chipmunks and moles with the BB gun Andy has given him, all of us fearful for him because he has no natural enemies to restrain him here. But he also turns out to be our best log splitter, flourishing the ax over his head like a demon and bringing it down in precise blow after blow, and then stacking the logs lovingly. On his own and freely, he distills the pain of Jennie's abandonment and begins to change it into something else, something all his own, busies himself with things that need doing, saving himself in this slow and tyrannical way, monster of his own devising, ruling over himself with an iron fist until he is able to leave the island of his pain and visit the peopled shore again. One summer he will paint our porch, working silently and alone for days. The rest of us descend to the beach in a cluster, and return hours later in the same cluster to him looking up at us with a broad smile. He prunes the lower branches of the trees near the house as far as he can reach, the rising apron encircling us matching his height plus the length of his arms. And swipes the cocoons of the gypsy moths in the tree tops with kerosene using a long pole.

When my cousins are grown, they'll all move back to this area, Marie alone, then the two boys together, as if returning to the scene of an unsolved crime to bear witness to all the unanswered questions. Their relationship with mama will be complicated, and she will keep a certain distance. But with me there will be no such hesitation, they are my blood brothers and sister always. And one day Ed will decide to become a medical doctor. Imagine that. And we both, Marie and I, will believe he can. He's smart enough. But if he manages to, it will only be because of what Marie does for him in the years after Jennie dies.

Between Andy and his three children there is some tenseness and a grim closeness. They do not blame him, but of course he blames himself and of course also he cannot help but blame Jennie for ushering him into her world and then not keeping her side of the deal. And in the end it isn't the children but Andy who turns away, which is a great loss to the children but a relief too even if a painful one, something they endure with terror and disbelief and yet which obviously benefits them too. To mama and me the strange combination of lucky and misfortunate that we have always found in my cousins never changes. They are still, to us, the fortunate ones. In the short time she was their mother, Jennie blessed them with a love like few children ever receive, and which even the shock of her death does not remove.

~

The winter after Jennie dies, when the seams of the world come unglued and for awhile the big brown house is just an old woodpile, and in the corner of our days the sun and the moon and the stars lie in a pile of darkness and the boulders and the trees and all the dirt and the water are in another pile, everything thrown down and shapeless, and the heart goes out of the world, I feel the weight of the words I carry like still water sloshing in a pail, too much for my skinny arms to lift and carry. I stand here, waiting and wanting, sitting in my little boat or in bed or on the top step of the front porch, wanting and waiting, knowing full well that whatever it is I'm waiting for has already come and gone.

I have a stepfather for awhile. George lives with us until just before Christmas—more than three whole months—and I'm grateful that he stays as long as he does considering how unhappy mama is because of Jennie. That must not have been easy for him. Leaving us is hard, too. And he doesn't go far. Just a half mile downstream along our brook, and up West Shore Road, to a summer cottage he rents year round, basking through the summers and shivering through the winters, where from his windows he looks out on the same sky and the same slow waters as we do. I even think I see more of him after he moves out. It is different for mama, but even she understands. He isn't leaving us for another woman or another anything. George leaves, if for any particular reason, because mama makes him feel like new disappointments come sprouting out of him every day. Moving out is his way of lowering our expectations and actually that part works out fine. And anyway, he isn't even my real stepfather, that is just what we call him so people won't talk.

After George leaves, he still comes by to spend time with me. He and I play cards sometimes at the dining room table. Mama stays up in her room the whole time, and after an hour or so it becomes awkward for George to be there feeling like he's confining her like that and he goes. Other times, especially if it's the end of the day, we might go, the two of us, to stand beside our bridge in the hopes of catching a glimpse of a beaver or even a black bear by the brook in the shadows and the half-light, since that's the hour and the place where you might see them.

I watch over mama, or try to, with a devoted daughter's love and concern. But I don't always want her to see me watching over her. There is in me a wariness that wasn't in me before. I'm keeping my eye out for signs now. Not so I'll be ready to run to her when she needs me, but so I'll have plenty of time to get out when the choice becomes saving myself or drowning with her. I'm starting to prepare myself, not planning my escape exactly, but steeling myself in earnest for the day that will come, when we're both a little older, when I'll be on my own, too.

Mama and I are both changing, thank God, even if the price of that is how nothing seems to go with our old closeness anymore. She begins taking classes up at Plymouth State, which is only twenty minutes from our house, even with her driving slowly like she does. There are textbooks spread out across the floor of the back room downstairs that she's always called her study but is now her study for real—the works of John Dewey and Herbert Read, Herbert Marcuse and Witold Grotowski, education theorists, arts educators, liberators—their spines split open to lay them flat, a little like mama were tearing the words out and eating them. When I come and open the door and look at her and then past her out the window of her little back room, the back fields silent, it feels to me as if we've taken those fields, packed them into cartons, and stacked the boxes for storage in the barn, so far-off do they seem all of a sudden. But I also feel her excitement. She's digging her way out, trying to.

I turn thirteen feeling like an old woman for whom March means maybe spring will come this year or maybe it won't. Mama spends fewer days sick in bed now. She's returned to me like a less physical version of herself, not a ghost, but more a spirit, her attachment to me stronger than her desire to be done with everything, though only for now, and not by much.

The first time she lets me go with her to a class, I sit next to her in the front seat of our Dodge station wagon, the windshield huge, almost like a magnifying glass distorting the empty stretches of countryside around us, making them seem suddenly unimaginably distant. Buoyed by my nearness to her, I believe again in her as a calm, self-assured, and potent presence. I'd forgotten how wise, funny, and youthful she can be when she wants. I see she's found her stride again. And in class I think she's smarter, more elegant and more beautiful than any of the other students. I can't understand why they don't take more notice of her. Anything seems possible for her—everything seems possible. And this time the blossoming I see in her is something she too feels. Like we are on a voyage, with no use for Ashland and Willow Lake anymore. And my only hesitation, my only fear, is that someday mama will leave me behind in the same way, with that same hunger for something else that makes her devour her textbooks the way she does. But that day still seems a long way off and I can live with it.

Sometimes, in the evenings, mama announces that she's going to have a bath. I understand exactly what she means: I am going to save myself. The next hour will be for no one but me myself and I. And whatever happens out here while the bath is running, the steam rising, no sounds in my ears but the water splashing against the sides of the tub—whatever happens out here will not touch me. Almost as if to say, Her Majesty the Queen of England is a woman, and so am I.

I don't like to interrupt her baths. I feel encouraged by

them, however symbolic and funny and domestic they may be. I understand that she's trying to establish boundaries as an exercise in self-strengthening, and I even understand, and accept, that probably the main thing she needs to protect herself from is me. I let her be driven once again, finally, or maybe I should say, for the very first time, by self-love, and this makes me more hopeful of my own chances.

And sometimes I do quietly go in and sit next to her there on a footstool beside the tub. But only to speak to her of things that really matter to me and when I do these are special occasions, and it's always with a feeling that I'm entering a sacred space she's made for herself.

Starting in 1978, when I was six, mama has worked Mondays, Tuesdays and Fridays at the Ashland branch of the Meredith Savings Bank. She also helps out sometimes at other places in town, either the Five and Dollar or the Ashland Laundromat. We don't pay the taxes on the big brown house. My father's mother looks after them so far as we know. We don't ask her about it, or thank her. But it's understood, and I know she feels better doing it than if she didn't. We'd be lost if we had to do it. Without the taxes, we don't need much to live. Mama makes do with what she earns working part-time. Most of it goes to keep the car running, and we need that.

Ever since I turned eleven, which was more than two years ago, I've been keeping a diary. Sometimes I write stories with happy endings for good people. I also started to write poetry, very seriously. But at the age I am, nothing makes sense to me, and I have stopped writing too.

I miss Marie. I think she and her brothers are better off than me now, since they have each other, whereas I'm more alone without them. I resent that, and in a way I miss Marie even more than

I miss Jennie, and that seems awfully unfair since Marie and the boys are alive and well somewhere. I beg mama to adopt them. The truth—though she doesn't tell me for years—is that she offered to. Of course she did. But the all-knowing State of New Hampshire considered her to be an unsuitable foster parent by comparison with the elderly couple in Pennsylvania, strangers who live in a different world from us.

I am beginning to discover what words mean to me. I am thirteen and the real starting point is my sense that all is lost.

Everything bad that could have happened has happened. Well, not everything, but so much. And yet everything goes along just the same. I come to know worlds within worlds. Whenever I see the face of a living thing, it astonishes me. As winter loosens its hold in April and then is forgotten as the months march on and my spindly legs find strength in them they didn't have before, I'm always investigating the faces of animals. I take Julius's head in both my hands to look deeply into her eyes, talking to her soothingly to see if in her eyes there might be the light of understanding.

All the animals have eyes that meet mine and hide nothing. Raccoons caught in the glare of our headlights. Loons on the water. Even the blind moles have eyes, or eye holes, that sparkle and tremble. I want to know how we're different. What kind of talking animals are we, exactly? I come to suspect that we're the only animals that purposefully deceive themselves. Were it not for our foolery, we'd be pursuing suicidal intentions most of the time, maybe all the time. The main thing, I decide, that we like to fool ourselves about is how our thoughts and our words are identical when, it's obvious to me, in fact our thoughts and our words lead separate lives. In our thoughts we fool ourselves utterly. In our words sometimes a truth or revelation that's larger than us pops out and we let it lie, large and astonishing, making us see.

On rare but memorable occasions, mama drinks too much wine at dinner and then holds forth. Before long she's sobbing her heart out, how my real father was only a boy, hadn't understood her, hadn't understood her at all, and could I even imagine the painfulness of that? Then, like she's still talking about the same thing, how real loneliness isn't like anything words can ever describe, how real loneliness is like a wild animal biting into your flesh.

On these long evenings the person she reaches out to isn't me but George, who lives nearby. She tries to get him to come over and sit with us at the dining room table. And sometimes he does come, out of politeness, but only to stay a short time. With embarrassment written on his kind round face, George pries himself loose after a little while, and I don't blame him. And then, after he leaves, I minister to her like I'm one of Snow White's dwarfs, bustling about her, completely attentive.

Then we are upstairs in the bathroom. After she has vomited, but is still drunk and inconsolable, I just wait with her, doing nothing while she rages on, enduring it with her. When finally she is quieter, I help her wash up. And then finally I lean her into my shoulder in the bathroom and lead her across the landing to her bed, where I sit with her until she falls asleep. Then I call George to let him know she's asleep at last, not knowing what else to say. He hardly says a word either, leaving to me the burden of her helplessness. As useless as I might be, sitting there on the stairs, whispering into the phone, I'm her only defender now against her troubles. I hang up. I have no one else to call. I wonder if this is it, if she's finally gone crazy. But looking after her on such a night seems not the worst imaginable thing, better than what it would be like if I had to look out for myself without her.

The next morning, she is perfectly fine again. No, she is better off for her outpourings of the night before, and I feel betrayed, exactly as I would if I were on a playdate and another child had gotten me to play a game and then changed the rules.

Mama will never get over losing Jennie, the hardness of it rolling over her and changing her, again and again. Her anger gives birth to a whole cosmology of anger towards men who had nothing to do with Jennie's death. But they are the accidents of mama's own life that left her unable to take better care of her younger sister, she feels, a sister who always found the time to take good care of her and us. What happened to Jennie could never happen to a man.

She speaks softly to herself out loud, knowing that I can hear every word and that I'm listening. Men are dogs, they need love but can't give love. Strays, mostly incapable of love and even more dangerous when they do love. Fear men in love more than anything, she tells herself. And when she says that, and looks up at me, that's when we both understood that she's talking to me after all.

And then there is something else, something she wants me to understand though she never comes out and says it. Just that, notwithstanding her own troubles and eccentricities she has managed to save herself and me for awhile but it would have been impossible for her to have saved Jennie too. She wants me to know this more than anything, because it means she doesn't trust her love anymore the way she used to, and in our little world this was real news that had to be shared.

Mama has prescriptions for sleeping pills, but doesn't take them. And then, not long after we lost Jennie, mama falls and hits her head and loses consciousness briefly. The doctor over in Plymouth says she had a concussion, and prescribes a different kind of pill. And again, mama doesn't take them.

At some point, I start taking one of the sleeping pills a few times a week, in the morning. And later I try the other one too, usually at night, when I'm up reading after mama goes to sleep. The names of the drugs are Seconals and Quaaludes, and the truth is that I really like them both. I don't think the doctor understands what these drugs are, how pleasurable they are. Doctors just prescribe them because there is this idea out in the world that drugs prescribed by doctors help people. Mama has no use for them, but to me, they offer a spiritual service, an inward turning excursion that is dangerous *and* healing. I think I understand all this a lot better than the doctor does. It makes sense to me somehow that a medication would be prescribed to mama that is intended by God for me, to help me endure. I cannot explain to you what it is to be a *young adult*—one of my favorite expressions, by the way, since it is plainly accurate in its description of the situation in which I find myself, since no one is ever exactly young when they're being adult, or adult when they're being young, but here I am, a young adult in fact, moving about in an open landscape that is suddenly not the unending one it used to be, but different—although it hasn't changed, only I have. And these mind-numbing drugs, Seconals, Quaaludes—dangerous and harmful, yes, but also my introduction to consciousness, since they show me it can be altered. And to the possibility of intention, since they can be weaponized towards harm, as Jennie has shown us, but can also reconcile us towards peace and tranquility. Those aren't the words I want. Not p & t but to time passing more like it actually does, timelessly. Time passing timelessly. I thought it might be so, and want to know for sure.

A little more than a year after Jennie dies, in September 1985, I decide I want to plant trees on our beach. Mama is encouraging. I settle on willows, for their swaying arms, and how they seem at home out in the open, near water. But I am divided in my own mind. To plant trees is to choose to be present in the future. And so, I agonize and second-guess myself. This isn't the right time of year. Spring would be better. Will the roots take hold in the two or so months to come before the ground freezes?

I'm willing to risk it, picturing in my mind's eye how it will be next summer when I row out into the lake towards the morning sun in my glass-bottom boat, facing backwards, the beach of spreading willows receiving the sun's rays as they recede from me, step by step, growing ever-smaller the further out I go, moved by the breeze, the willows of my dreams and desires, the ripples in the water between us turning like lathes. And later, to return to see the hanging boughs of my spreading willows, splendid and peaceful, suspended over the beach, perhaps filled with swallows and goldfinches, their quick passages from branch to branch speaking the language of restlessness, of earnestness, of things mattering terribly to them. Against the slow waxing and waning of light and color, dignified and hopeful, architect of its own erasure, the relief of that too. Such peace, though it is intermittent. Every time I escape on to the lake there's the possibility that by the time of my return I'll have discovered some secret passageway out of our troubles.

Mama drives me east along the old highway, Rte 3, to the nursery, a little house set all around with plants of all shapes and sizes, mostly thriving, leaves thrusting, chest out, like men at a wedding, blooming annuals set out on spindly tables in a riot of color, all the different growing shapes and colors set against the silent backdrop of the vast forest and low mountains that begin just after the little lawn and driveway. The woman helps me find the two willow saplings wrapped in wire, the main roots bulging from the root sacks like heads hanging upside-down, and the smaller roots, ghostly white, that remind me of little fingers, clusters of them all intertwined. The man lifts the saplings into our car, one at a time. And we drive away with the trunk tied open and the car ass low and the trees swaying behind us in what I decide is their happy dance.

Arriving home we drive straight down to our beach and set about digging the holes, working at last in the yellow sand that always seems to need something more from us. I count twenty-two steps from the water and choose two spots about twenty-two steps from each other.

In the end it takes mama and me two days, and then we back our Dodge Rambler station wagon right over each hole and set about freeing the willows and letting them fall in, and then pour in bucket after bucket of water and then we add the dirt and sand until there is a kind of burial mound around each trunk.

At no time does it ever seem quite right. Even once the saplings are in the ground they look like something sticking up that doesn't belong. That isn't something that will ever change. But they look awfully good to me even so, after all the work we did. You can be proud of anything if it costs you enough.

Before the first frost, one of the trees is brought down and dragged off by the beavers. I buy chicken wire in town and loosely double-wrap the trunk of the second one so the same thing doesn't happen to it too. Through the winter I think incessantly about the tree planted there as lifelessly as a pole in the ground. And in the spring, I carry down a kitchen chair to stand on, and shears as long as my arm, and prune the dead branches off it.

I do that every year still, about a month after my birthday, but with a folding ladder now and even then the higher branches are beyond my reach. Her trunk is now nearly nine inches thick, and gnarled, scarred and pockmarked.

And though my willow stands, the short walk to it sometimes feels to me like a tremendous voyage across a vast distance. She is part of me—and so reaching her is one of the most difficult journeys. She drinks in the sun, stands on her own, stands solitarily where the intention had been for her to be one of two. She grows from year to year, but instead of spreading her arms as I imagined she would, she extends them upwards little bit by little bit. Her leaves are sickly, and too many of the branches die each year. The bark of the trunk is riddled with the small drill-holes of the woodpeckers that flock to her. And I know no way to protect her from them. But even so she grows taller and bigger, and stronger, with each passing year.

I will not write, In her aloneness, or, In her solitude. But on the other hand, You are never alone is just a phrase. Believing you are not alone makes it so. But the opposite is true, too. You stand here, alone and all but abandoned. One true thing neither cancels out nor changes the other. All alone, never alone. I stand twenty-two steps from my surviving willow tree, right where her sister that perished was, marking the spot. I'm smoking of course, puffing away. The first drag is like a gust of the freshest wind passing through me. Nothing can compare. After that, the rest of the cigarette has the taste of ashes. My words are sparrows and starlings darting here and there, leaving no trace of their passage.

Andy (1984)

Boudreau, Proulx, Paquette. French Canadian. And then the Anglo ones, Avery, Scott, Blake. The only Indian names left here are on bodies of water, Pemigewasset, Winnipesaukee and the others, traces that remain.

More often than not, wars were fought in other places, down in Massachusetts, or up in Montreal. Great battles in the Revolutionary War, and in the War of 1812 between America and Britain, when the Crown burned Washington, DC to the ground and our side beat them back up in Canada. And in what they call the Sixty Year war, which lasted from before the American Revolution to well past the end of the Civil War and that was the war of eradication of the Indian nations.

New Hampshire boys volunteered and organized into companies and marched down to Mass or up to Canada to fight. The Civil War took many New Hampshire sons, dozens from Ashland alone. There's a Civil War monument in town to prove it. We've given our share of blood to every war that was. The Vietnam War took men I knew and looked up to, who mostly came back changed from the experience, mentally and physically. But on our own New Hampshire soil the real wars we fight are against our winter cold, sometimes flash floods in warm months, and against our own selves suffering the hardships of our freedom-loving isolationism you could say.

The state used to be all field from the Massachussets border to here where I'm standing, and mostly forested from here northward, through the Great White Mountains right up to the

Canadian border. And there was no highway, only Rte. 3 and little roads, so you passed through every town and had to go easy on the gas pedal.

But, it's interesting—we're always traveling. That's New England. The weather is hardly the same from one week to the next and that's what we're used to. It's only the people that mostly don't change, I mean not in their nature. And now, to me, it's like we're always moving in two opposite directions at the same time. We're forested again because there's little farming here left to speak of, so there hasn't been a good reason to do the work of keeping up the fields and as the forest encroaches, we let it. Walk through all the forested acreage around here and you step over stone walls pretty much everywhere. They settle into themselves mostly, and endure. If they erode, it also strengthens them, even though they never used mortar to make them, just stones on top of stones. But the way it's done they last for the ages. And that's the proof. Every time you pass a stone wall in the forest it means the land was a field once, livestock grazed here, rows of corn stood, and the winter sun hit the bare ground, with a little pocket of trees here around a boulder, there bordering a stream. Is there anything as beautiful as that? You tell me. And when you clear a rock-infested field as we've all done at one time or another, you build a wall out of the stones you've dug up and make a thing of beauty out of the necessity of it.

So much is different. We're in a modern world now, where corn is grown in Iowa and potatoes in Idaho and livestock are grazed in Montana and butchered in Chicago. The change has come to us but we still haven't changed much.

It's three miles to town from the home where I was born. There were fields of NH corn growing alongside the road in most fields, and by late June it was a high wall of lime green I couldn't see over. The lines of apple trees, two or three across and endlessly long followed the lay of the land, cresting the hills and sweeping down into the lowlands, dappled with light. To the south of us, people point their noses towards Boston and the jobs there, places of industry, and to the north of us, it's forestry and the timber trade mostly. And here we're not exactly part of either group. They call us the Lakes Region, but that's for vacationers coming up from Massachusetts. To ourselves, we're people that can look both ways and see what we see. The timber industry can employ us, the summer residents also. We can go off to fight in wars. But we're from a place that isn't just one thing or the other.

Farming has always been a philosphical question here, what with our winters and the rockiness of the soil. When I say a philosophical question what I mean is, you can't win, you never can win, so that's where the philosophy comes in. My people farmed a little, but were always looking for other work too, hungry for it.

We worked in the mills in town some, and in the bigger mill towns north of us, good, dirty work, hard work, dangerous work you were proud to do. My people looked north with admiration, though mostly we wanted a softer life. When you went up there, to Littleton and the other mill towns, the air and water by the mill were poisonous, the people were boisterous, they were tough up there. The danger, bringing down the logs in the spring, riding the logs, kids did some of that work but you had to be strong. Money was being made and a few families, the mill owners, made a lot of it. It wasn't like today where the profits just mostly disappear. Back then they took some, and some they used to build up the factory, to build the schools and the recreation facilities and the churches. The mill towns were where you went if you could to see a good doctor, and to get a pretty good education. And Ashland had one of the first paper mills in all of New Hampshire. We had pride in the town's industry back then. We were off the beaten track, though that changed somewhat after 1964 when the interstate reached us. We were thankful that the winters weren't quite as harsh here as they can be in the north of the state, a little closer to the southern New England states which we considered soft, and we thought of ourselves as tough, a lot tougher, but still touched by the southern softness too.

Some people go to church and feel a little tug, women mostly. Because it's theatrical. The pastor knows how to put his little finger inside you, touching on hopes and the pull of the eternal, which is death itself, faceless but still attractive. In my family, we have mostly lived long and modestly. But in each passing generation there was a little mischief stored up, some trouble-making ability saved from one generation to the next, and after about six generations that stored up demonology was born in me.

I want to say, there's a reason why we are how we are. There's always a reason. For me, I think it has something to do with my ma. Something about how she was with me, different from with my older brother or pa. There was always a dissatisfaction in me, and she understood that it was because I was smart. It was something in me that was real, some kind of bitterness, and she respected it, I don't know how else to say it.

Even as a kid, I knew what there was that I was proud of in the life here. I'd tasted it, seen it growing up. And I somehow knew it had been taken from us. I knew that there had been a time, and not too long ago either, when we were proud of who we were here. When you could stretch out your arms in two directions, to the east and to the west, and feel that you were a man here in the same way that a tree is a tree or a boulder a boulder. There was plenty of everything. Just like, now still, I can go to Crystal Springs and fill my plastic jugs with pure mountain spring water by right, no charge for that, it's clear spring water that belongs to us all, as much as you want. Everything—a lot of things—were at least a little like that. The land and the water. You could go swim in a lot of places, and the air was clear and bracing, still is. The white pine that grew in the woods was not in limited supply. You knew there was back-breaking work, up north, all you wanted, timbering for the paper mills in those northern towns. And if you didn't go there it was because you didn't have to, because there were easier things you could do closer to home, things less prone to the kind of injuries that happened up north. Of course boys joined up and went off to fight. But even that, you were paid for it and if you came back injured you were taken care of. Many of our families sent one son off, and some sent two. And even if you came back in a wheelchair the life before you, a life of contemplation, on disability, in the company of your parents, well, that wasn't a good life you can say, but even that life, back then, it got you respect, had dignity in it. That changed after Vietnam of course. Those boys were still part of something here though, had stories to tell too, stories we took at face value and they weren't criticized for having put themselves in harm's way like they were in other places.

There was an activity for every tick in the clock of the year. If it wasn't tapping the sugar maples for syrup in March and April, when the nights are still below freezing but the days can be warm, it's the smelt running in May, along with the corn planting, the strawberry harvest in June, then the peaches, the corn harvest started in August and then the apple harvest too that runs through October. All the carpentry work you could ever want all summer long. New Hampshire isn't a populous state, unless you're counting trees. There was always as much work as an able-bodied man could ever want.

So is it a wonder we are left with some anger and bitterness now for the things that have been taken from us, with little trade-off, little to show for it, just scraps really?

The construction of the I-93 highway changed things. It didn't happen in a day. In fact, it took more than thirty years to finish it, and a lot of people didn't want it. The old road, Rte. 3, came north and you could go forty or fifty miles an hour, and pass through towns from Nashua on up, stopping at street lights. I-93 inched a few miles at a time all through the sixties and seventies, reaching Ashland I think in 1964. Now it's a super-highway I guess you could call it. Hasn't done us much good, but it's meant a lot to all the people that come and go.

I'm 34. Jennie married me when the little one, Harold, was only five weeks old. It was like finishing the thought that was born when Jennie and I first laid eyes on each other, whenever that was. I guess she must have been thirteen and me twenty-one. And it was probably on the wall under the six spreading oak trees right outside the high school, unless it was on the other wall where we congregated, under the town library in the town center. She came up with her older sister. I was on the look-out for someone just like her, an Ashland girl looking up at me ready for anything and everything. After that . . . well, we were good and we were happy mostly. We should never have gotten married. Afterwards, I was on her side in her dissatisfaction with it. I don't know why or how, but it changed me some-how, or changed us. I wish now we'd just stayed as we were, though maybe that's the one thing people don't ever get to do. We married at her sister's house. She was 22 and I'd just turned 30. Our oldest, Marie, was eight, same as her cousin Carolyn. We didn't stay married long, not even to the end of that year. And the break-up isn't anything I would hold against Jennie either. What was marriage to us, when we already knew how we wanted to be? When she broke the news to me that it was over I was almost relieved at first. I thought it would be a return to how we were before, not a break-up. I still wanted to buy her the house so that she'd never have to leave it unless she wanted to, I wanted that security for her at least. And she accepted that, and I kept making the payments. That's all I could think about, not that we were breaking up. Unmarried was our most natural state. It didn't mean we were going to be any different from how we'd always been really, not to me anyway. The kids were going to be okay. None of them needed me around all the time, so long as they knew they could call on me any time. The fact was, the way that worked best for us was just how it had been from the beginning. But there must have been a lot I didn't know about my Jennie, a whole world of things. Now why was it like that? I'll never know, but I imagine it's a thing that goes back for centuries, and directly to Jennie's mom at least, and the life that was torn up and thrown away when she fled Europe after the tanks rolled in to silence an uprising she was caught up in along with a hundred thousand or so other students so I understand, and ever further back I imagine. To things that aren't known or spoken about, but still are like a hidden hand guiding what happens to us.

I still imagine two people happy together. And the children happy around them. And he has work, and she has the work of the home, and maybe earns a little at the cash register somewhere a few days a week. And the life of the family is in the countryside and a little in town, where the kids start school, one after the other, where her part-time job is, and where he goes to the lumbar yard for tools or sawed timber to build with from time to time, all of it fitting together like a jigsaw puzzle laid out on the table, not a single piece missing.

With Jennie gone, I couldn't raise them on my own. I had to let them go to others that could. That hurt, but it was the right thing and I knew it, and I don't think the kids themselves ever thought otherwise or held it against me either.

The wildness around here isn't just a wildness out there. It is part of our sense of order. The killing cold all through the worst winter months, and how we circle inside larger orbits of a vastness. And when a tree falls, or a crack appears and then you see a round boulder split into three and collapse all of a sudden, like a man having a heart attack . . . well, it works the other way too. And once I did see a man have a heart attack and keel over and it did remind me of a slab of granite breaking up. You feel it inside you. We're made of flesh, but we're made of stone and fir tree too. So when grief strikes, as it has stricken me, God knows, we always endure and at the same time, whether from grief or just the hardship of things passing from one thing into the next, or from some conversion of the two, we also bow our heads and relent, like it's a crime that won't ever be solved. And the funny part is just how sometimes you can't tell which is the sweet part and which the bitter, or even if it isn't the sweetness that really kills you. I think of Jennie all the time, and when I think of all her many problems and flaws I can smile and think of her without sadness somehow. But when I think of all the ways she was a perfect companion, and all the ways she could look ahead and see our future all laid out in a way that was real and decent and good for us, all the ways she was my beloved and good to me, and I can hear her like a note in music that doesn't waver but doesn't strain or falter either, it's the good in her, the part that is still so alive to me, it's that sweetness that makes me feel like I can't go on.

Part Seven

Carolyn (1978)

When I start going to school, walking down our road at the start of those days is a tremendous undertaking for me. Mama comes out on to the porch and scrutinizes the sky to hide her own struggle, and then she waves one last time, without looking at me, and goes back inside. Then it is silence behind me, deafening silence all around. Just the stirring of the wind in the trees and the sun painting the topmost branches, while down below, even as I walk away I nestle in the dampness for as long as I can, hanging back even as I walk forward, staying a little longer near our forgiving fields.

Julius, my short legged and excitable beagle and collie mix, named after Orange Julius, which is orange juice with creamy fizz, accompanies me every morning to a point halfway between our house and the road, and will go no further. There she plants herself, watching me walk the rest of the way, taking each daily departure as our final parting, a last good-bye, inconsolable to see me leave forever. I wait for the dirty orange bus to stop across from our mailbox with a terrible sense of having fallen from grace.

And in the afternoons, when Julius sees me return up the road, she rejoices over my unforeseen deliverance, running madly in circles, then throwing herself against my legs with her full force, sometimes knocking me over, and then licking my face as I let myself fall back into the embrace of grass, trees, sky, and granite, the sound of water flowing if it is spring, and the rasping sound of dry leaves spinning in the wind if it is fall, the air's electricity, and finally mama standing on the porch like a bird in a cage, waiting for me, free neither with nor without me.

As I return up the long road to our house I already recognize the look on her face even before I am close enough to her to see it, the look that admits nothing, that acts light-hearted even though her love for me is tormenting her.

And then her turning away that says without words that I will always come and go, that this is my right, that whether good or bad comes to me it is all the same to her and the end of us, and whether this produces grief or immense relief no part of her face, so expressive sometimes, reveals, since, of course, as I know now, it is both these things.

You may as well take the good with the bad, since both the good and the bad will take you whatever you do. Words I never hear her say, but in my head when I hear them the voice I hear say them is hers. All that's left to me to add is Amen.

Yet even so, mama's quietness comforts me, a silence recognizably ours among all the other silences. Comforts me because she's all I have, and because in her way she's as strong as anyone or anything around us.

Every tree has its own quivering ring of soundlessness, like an energy field, and every boulder breaking the surface of the fields, too. The sky presses down, and the sound of running water strokes the air like a keeper of silences. But it seems to me that mama's quietness in the middle of all this is cunning and sharp as anything.

Had she been louder and more playful, more often angry, more assertive, she would have been drowned out somehow, not by other people maybe, but by this place we have found. Keeping to herself like she does, she's become a force equal to any other. She always has an athlete's grace, and when we walk together and she rests her slender arm on my shoulder and plays with my hair we seem to me to be an unbeatable team.

I am the voice of her silences. I feel that so strongly, grateful that she has left this to me, that she has left me so much to say for her, our time together mostly quiet like it mostly still is, the effect on me a mixing together of sweetness and sorrow, sweetness and sorrow.

We pay for our groceries with cash and pale pink food stamps the girl counts and sorts wearing a mild grimace that shows, not that she cares, but at least that she has noticed us, which is something even if not much. Mama stands half-facing her and half-facing me, her mouth in a sort-of pout, her body wired together, weak in the knees, as if, not yet a woman, she feels she has to give up what little strength she has, holding my hand and squeezing, and me squeezing back, my legs planted firmly, knowing that even as a little child I am stronger than her, and that only one of us has to be strong.

So, from the very beginning of our life together, we begin casting the lines between us that aren't erasable, she counting on me already to steady her and me pulling her every which way.

Our closeness right from the start, from even before I can remember, from the very, very beginning. But, at the same time, something else, almost the polar opposite of our closeness: me knowing I am holding her here against her will, against herself, when she'd be better off without me, living her own life. Knowing that. That being the first thing I ever knew. And although she willingly lets me, lets herself be kept here suspended in mid-step or mid-song, this doesn't change the fact that she is only waiting to return to her own journey—our life together just the pause between her girlhood and whenever she'll be getting back to where she left off when she was seventeen and I came along and interrupted her.

On the days when mama is working afternoons, sometimes I walk over after school to where she is, and I sit and watch her do the little things, making small talk with customers and with the other workers, and I am transfixed by the flat expansiveness of it all, silenced in some strange way, as the child of an employed person, both of us voiceless even though she does a good job at the talking part, and there's some relief in that.

Other days, she lets me take the bus home and I go find Julius and then the two of us walk down to Gordon and Edith's until mama comes and gets us. Julius and I go right into Gordon and Edith's cabin without knocking first, the dogs funhouse for awhile while we all watch, and then we just lay about and settle in.

Gordon and Edith met when they were only a little older than mama is now, and fell in love at the same time as they both were sickly and being treated for the same life-threatening condition that took their breath away. Edith had it worse than Gordon did, but their growing love was stronger. Mama makes it sound very romantic. And you can just imagine how much it means to us to think that right near us we have these friends who were not overcome by life's adversity, but met it head on together and in their low-key way somehow triumphed.

They made their home in Tucson, Arizona, and New Mexico before coming here, and could have chosen to be anywhere in the world. But out of all the places they went to, including New Zealand, they chose their small cabin on Willow Lake. Edith says that, of all the places they were, only our lake is an inhabitable paradise.

Edith is even skinnier than I am. Gordon too. She only paints her watercolors out of doors. I watch from any spot I can find near her, not too far, but not too close either. In every finished picture our world is so alive it breathes. She's that good. Anybody who sees them says so. Standing beside her, looking out on the lake with her, watching her paint, is like not having skin between me and everything else.

Sometimes Edith and I go out on to her dock, the mile-long lake before us, our scrawny mountains and the tin roofed sky above, and the wind blowing in our ears. We make a game of listening for the word for the only thing that lasts forever, without knowing yet what the word might be, hoping we'll recognize it when we hear it. Oh, how we listen—and in our game the word in the wind is always changing.

One minute we hear, Nothing! The next, Sky. Or, Ants! Funny words but never the ones we're wishing for.

We hope that after these words are done the ones we want to hear will come.

Gordon is only a little taller than Edith is, with a slight stoop when he walks and a nose with a pretty curve to it exactly like a falcon's beak. He has his pottery studio in the crawl space under their house, where he at first uses a kick wheel he made himself out of a heavy round grinding stone, a steel pole, and a potting wheel on top that is the only prefabricated part. But by now he pots on an electric wheel, and uses the older one for turning and glazing. He has a kiln in the corner, and shelves along the wall beside it filled with big opaque plastic jars for the glazes he mixes. He makes perfect pots in shapes that seem to come out of the earth in the way roots do. Well-made pots, thin-walled and light, practical and handsome, in colors of dirt and rotted leaves but luminous. Gordon's pots don't look man-made. He says that man-made things didn't usually inspire him artistically. Holding one of his pots, you can see thinking didn't make it, but feeling what it is not to be human, not builder but stone, not hunter but footfall. Years later, I will actually say something like that to Gordon, the years giving me the understanding and then the words, bringing him those words, the freshness and hardness of them, and he will light up like a Christmas tree.

I don't always understand the things Edith says to me when she's painting her watercolors and leans over to tell me something, but I remember them and sometimes I repeat them to myself out loud. Not understanding the things she says isn't a problem for me with Edith.

With watercolors, she says, you just have to go with whatever happens.

Another time, I am looking at how what we can see is joined together to what we can't see. I don't understand, but I love her way of stringing nonsensical things together without changing their nonsensicalness.

She also says, Colored water on paper is my all and my everything. It makes me happy to think that something so close to nothing can be all and everything to her.

Another time she tells me, Watercolors only whisper. And, again, without knowing what she means exactly, I'm happy that she's confiding in me things I know she isn't saying to anyone else, not even to Gordon. And I understand it's so that, much later, if ever I want to, I can recall our time together the way you get an old box of toys out from under the bed and find all the pieces still there in the box where you left them all those years ago.

She talks to Gordon with a strange mixture of affection and skepticism. Not that she doesn't love him—I knew she does, very much—but she needs her space.

Once Edith tells me the story of Joan of Arc and how Saint Joan turns everything upside down, not caring what people think, believing in herself, believing God believes in her. And I'm very sad and surprised when in the end Joan dies in the story.

It seems different from what is supposed to happen.

It is to test the strength of our belief that it happens this way, and to remind us of our frailty, Edith says.

Maybe because Gordon and Edith's cabin is small and roughly made, it always appears to me to be shifting, never still, like a boat tied to a buoy. Often I arrive to the sounds of Gordon working coming up through the floorboards, and Edith seated in the shade somewhere outside nearby. I remember best the between times when she spends the long minutes sitting inside in a chair, hardly moving, looking out, doing nothing in particular, perhaps with a book in her lap, but not reading. And when I come in, she turns slightly towards me and then returns to her contemplation, her eyes red and unseeing. Then I sit as near to her as I can. We let the minutes and hours of the day inhabit us. In the watery progression we feel a tingling hesitancy everywhere around us. We weigh the dramatic possibilities in each passing moment. And we're never bored.

Andy (1989)

There's a picture of my great-grandfather standing on the deck of what looks to be a twenty-five- or thirty-foot steamboat on Squam River just before it enters Ashland, with a cast iron pot-belly stove behind him pumping and puffing away and the river all around so thickly strewn with the bobbing trunks of tall trees it looks like you could walk across the river on them. He's bearded all around the lower half of his face and is wearing a stiff cap with a visor and the expression on his face looks to me like he's laughing and stomping and making money and all is well. His face appears scarred, though it may just be a flaw in the photoprint. Either way, no one looking at this picture would ever confuse my great-grandfather for a man you could trifle with. I never knew him, except through his son and whatever part of his personality my pa also has. When you take a farmer and put him on a boat it can be like turning wild horses loose. I do know that although we were a family that farmed the land, we never exactly had the tranquility of farmers, ma didn't, and pa didn't either.

Ma and pa have been selling off pieces of our land ever since I can remember, and pa and I spend more time fixing up trucks and cars now than farming. I recognize in pa's eyes something indescribable, his own version of my anger and bitterness. But in him it's not angry or bitter, more of a crustiness and a curiosity, and a softness in him. Bless pa, he has a sense of humor like no one else I've ever met. He finds all the heartbreak something he can make fun of, even at his own expense sometimes. The human comedy isn't lost on him. He's not a man to read books. I doubt he's read even one in his whole life. But he knows he's got it good, doesn't need a book to tell him so. Inherited the house, and the land for a quarter-mile around it in all directions. He knows he can always sell an acre or two to pay the land taxes. He knows he married a good woman. How many people know when they have it good? Well, my pa does. He knows what the natural world will do on its own, and the things you can help it do, like planting and weeding, and he knows you don't have to steer it much to live off it. And he loves ma. Why wouldn't he?

Our apples fell to the ground. We harvested some, enough, more than enough. The rest the crows ate where they fell. Our fields were rough like churning seas, and instead of working in them every day, week after week, clearing and planting and harvesting, we only rode across them twice a year on the high seat of a tractor, dousing them in the fumes from the motor, and afterwards the aroma of fresh cut grass lingered, filled our nostrils for a day, and we left the long stalks where they fell, to turn yellow, and eventually the husks disintegrated into the ground or blew away.

Time doesn't stand still, ma says. So we stopped growing corn or anything much around the same time everybody else did. The local markets already had more local corn than they knew what to do with, and the kind that grew on the thousand-acre Midwestern farms was cheaper and more perfect and you could get it year-round. Even so, ma used to say it was a sickness not to grow things like we used to. The fence posts that had kept the livestock off the planted fields now lean drunkenly this way and that. The electric fence is still there, hanging loosely from post to post but we don't keep it electrified because there's no need.

Ma was always pretty. There's an expression I like, which is when we say of a woman that she is pretty like a deep cut, meaning hardship can bring a kind of beauty with it. Ashland girls are known around the region for being pretty, it is a witchery or black magic I could say. They're conscious of it, and humble about it, but it is a kind of power and they know it. But ma was a rough-cut jewel of an ageless descendance, with a kindness in her that shone through her eyes.

The funny thing is that pa was pretty too, in an old-Hollywood sort of way, gentlemanly, slow moving, not wordy, or citified, but country. Ma was his voice, and they were a good couple in that they did change each other for being part of each other, though maybe only I saw it. Pa knew what it was to plant in rocky ground, and to toil with your fingers in sub-zero temperatures, but he also knew how you can turn your back on that toil and take an easier stance. There is controlled insanity and how hard you can work if you don't stop yourself. Pa had instead the simple sanity of turning your back on that life and taking it a bit easier. And I think he did it for her, to give her an easier life, and it was her thoughtfulness that made him do it, at least I think so.

Pa is a methodical person, he's innately smart and has learned to be steady and not to rush things. There is an edge of philosophical-mindedness and more than a touch of cruelty in him too. Ma says that, she would know better than me. She also said to me once that the rock-infested ground and bitter winters beat our family down for generations and Harold has taken that curse off them. The nearly worthless land we inherited has become valuable in our lifetime. We've been fortunate. I listen to every word ma has to say on the subject, but then I think about it and I decide that whatever curse ever was here is here still, on ma and pa and me and my brother. Isn't that the meaning of a curse anyway, that it is always lurking somewhere nearby?

You could say our animals were expressions of this. Hens and cows are Godforsaken animals, like ma says, and our livestock and produce were no different, it seems to me, raised for production and slaughter. What is forsaken by God is for people to love. That's always been my idea of things, the one that has made the most sense to me for as long as I can remember. Those who are beloved of God don't need me. It's the other ones that need all the love we can find in our hearts to give them, starting with ma's hens and our cows and the dogs of course.

Ma's hens produce every night and in the morning she collects the eggs, several dozen usually. Ma sits at her kitchen table for a while in the early sun that comes in through her window on that side. And sometimes one of the neighbors walks over or drives up and buys a half-dozen or a dozen.

It was on the morning after a storm, when I came down and passed the egg cartons on the table, ma wasn't there. And then I saw her all spread out lying face down in her nightgown on her waxed and buffed floor, a picture of forlorn misery. I picked her up in my arms, called out to pa, but didn't wait. Outside I managed to open the door of my truck on the passenger side, and fastened her seatbelt tight around her so she'd stay sitting up. She had a pulse but not much of one and her breathing was slow and shallow like she were mostly gone already. She was unconscious but not relaxed, with an expression of concern on her sleeping face and in her body.

She stayed in the hospital for about a week. She was unconscious for the first three days. Pa and I would go there, but there wasn't anything we could do.

There wasn't much of a story. And I only heard it, years later, after pa died, and it was ma herself that told me. She had met a man, one of the summer people on the lake. The night before, she had told pa about it. It wasn't that she was leaving us, not yet anyway. It was that she was cast adrift in her own self, in her feelings and her sense of things. She did not know what pa would do, or what she would do. But she felt she had to tell him. And then, once she had, her sense of turmoil became something she simply could not endure, and sitting at her kitchen table in the early morning after getting the eggs she had tried to end her life.

What would pa have done if she hadn't done what she did, I mean tried to kill herself? Well, he wasn't going to do anything. I would have said so to her at the time if I'd known. But to me as I recount this now, well, telling him was something beautiful, and the way she did it also, without a plan I mean. In a way she was telling him nothing, that was the hard truth, unless it was just that there was another side to her, more to her, and she wanted him to know.

I'd seen ma with him once, on the road about halfway between our place and the lake. They were standing there holding hands, either parting or meeting up. There was something in their looks, intimacy, but more than that an openness as if they shared something no one could ever be ashamed of. I turned back around before they saw me.

Ma recovered. Everything went back to normal. If anything, ma seemed happier now. Pa was always the same. He straightens himself up when he has something to say, his eyes fix on the point in the distance where one of his mown fields meets the forest edge, his hand supporting his lower back where it hurts. His face is intent when he is listening to you. And after a while he says, I'll have a look, or, I know it!

Ma will say his name ten thousand times in the years to come, casting her spell over herself and him. Harold, Harold, or to me pa. The more times the more she believes in the good in him and in the good in herself too. His name as she says it takes on more dignity and weight over time, I swear it's true. As I have grown into the man I am, and they have grown older together, the voice that accompanies us is ma's, and the feel of pa's name as it forms in her mouth every time she says it is like a prayer, or even an answered prayer. She lets us hear the song inside her, and part of that is her surprise. She has found something in the end that she risked losing. She found it because she risked losing it. The feelings that came to her, late in the day, were ones she never expected to have.

It is strange, but they grew more romantic with time too, because in the end it is what they both wished for. And because they both forgave each other every trespass, including those that were not easy to forgive.

Ma is getting on now, she's one of the steady people, with her slightly crooked smile of concern, the same one that I saw on her unconscious face that day, now with librarian's glasses and proper gray hair. What's funny is that ma has a greater physical presence now. As she has gotten heavier with age, she holds herself in such a way as to be more imposing, broader in the shoulders and hips, still shapely but more confident and assertive. She has outlived her own frailty, and especially the frailty of her own uncertain emotions, her loneliness and doubt. With her ideas and her secrets my ma has come through in the end, a woman of rare character. As she always was, yes, but she has gone the distance and it means something.

My pa finally sold the last parcel of land, including the house, and ma and pa moved to a nice mobile home on flat acreage on the other side of town right on the Pemigewasset River, and took up farming again there in a modest way. We'd already moved my poor brother to the veterans hospital by then, and he would be the first in our family to die. I built my own place on a little piece of our ancestral land, across the road from the old house, and I have my own little family there now, my wife and child who never knew the younger me.

Pa passed. And so now ma is alone in the new place, and still works in town some and keeps things going on their new land.

When I see her she smiles at me as if to say in the end I have also brought her happiness after all, more than she expected I would, let's say. She dotes on the baby, and Marie and Ed and Harold go see her whenever they can get up here. She'll have to go into an assisted living home eventually, but not yet.

Ma is as kind as ever. She may not have much to do now, but she is thankful, and still can laugh at herself and entertain herself. I think she's grateful that nothing bad happened to me in the end that I wasn't able to recover from. Once I was in the Five and Dollar when she was working there, and a woman asked after pa, and I saw her harden a little before saying Harold had died. She doesn't lament anything that happened. She moves on and lives every day.

Part Eight

Carolyn (1992)

I'm reading a lot of poetry books. I find them to be deeply factual. Not narrative, not and then and then and then, stakes in the ground marking time's passage, and not impressionistic, as people assume poetry to be, but cleft stone and ice, factual in that way.

The Plymouth State College Library is to the Ashland Library what a helicopter is to a wheelbarrow. I'm sitting in the periodicals room one afternoon with the *Michigan Quarterly Review*, the Fall 1991 issue, where I discover a very long and winding—12 page!—poem called "My Mother's Nipples," about a young boy's mother's drunkenness, by a poet named Robert Hass:

I said to myself:
    Some things do not blossom in this life.

    I said: what we've lost is a story
    and what we've never had
    a song.

The poet returns again and again to this borderline between being and nonbeing as only a child considering its mother can:

    What we've never had is a song
    and what we've really had is a song.

A few lines later, still struggling for air:

> There are all kinds of emptiness and fullness
> That sing and do not sing.

And then there is this line:

> I said you are her singing.

The poem continues for another page, and then, just before the end, there are these lines,

> You are not her singing, though she is what's
> Broken in a song.
> She is its silences.

When she fishes with Gordon and sometimes her sisters in their handsome aluminum canoe, Edith's lips move slightly in response to whatever it is God happens to be saying to her, the look on her face always that of someone deep into something. She speaks only rarely and with great aforethought—a word she favors. Lips moving, I understand only now, because there are so many things that must be said that will never be said. Life's lived mysteriously in rapture or not at all.

We aren't fools, you know. I hear her say that once, chewing the words, looking straight ahead, her eyes still pools. She says it the way you do when you're saying something aloud that you've said silently to yourself a hundred times, fighting for the words to be as true in saying them as they were when you kept them in, wanting them to change everything in some small way at least.

My Edith always sees, and wants to know everything that's happening to her, eyes wide open to the bitter end to taste the dregs, like a still life water color painting of herself, but as a spectator now. Nineteen-ninety-two is the year of her aphelion.

Her cataracts have become so pronounced that she has stopped painting. Her eyes aren't the only thing ailing her, but are probably what affects her spirit the most. Her doctor has determined them to be inoperable. I want to talk about it with her. We've always talked to each other about things. From the time I was four years old that's been our way. I ask her what it's like. There's no interpreting her sing-song voice now unless I put my ear right against her lips. She says, It is a tumultuous music.

She smiles at me, and clearly would prefer to say not another word on the subject. But I'm waiting. I'm not done with her yet. So she goes on. It is a thunderous music I still hear but can no longer share with you or anyone else. Now that she has completed her thought, she lets her old mouth form a grim line, momentarily not hiding anything from me.

Her pleasure seeing is only in memory now. And having confessed this much to me, she closes her eyes for a moment to regain her composure, after which we return to our sitting as if nothing whatsoever has been said between us on the subject of her approaching blindness. Whatever it is that enters in through her eyes now, whatever storm of color and light and wind, excites her memories but no longer stirs her to act. Not seeing, which she describes to me with fear in her eyes as A soft pounding, pounding, pounding, is new. But she continues to feel. There is still, she says, The great intoxication of my visual pleasure. Her memories flood in to fill the void, overwhelming her. She says, It is like being all alone in a movie theater, just a man who sits up there in the booth running the projector and me. It is wonderful and unbearable at the same time my dear.

Not working, not doing anything with her hands and her

spirit, no longer making something that only exists because she has brought it forth, she finds to be impossible. We are too selfish, she says, Unbearably selfish. I am trying, she says, to accept doing nothing. But dear God, how am I to understand?

I don't know her age and don't ask. Politely, tenderly, she tells me how, for her, not seeing anymore is another season. When you are young, the world has its eye on you, she says. The rest of the time, it turns away. And it is up to you to be the eye looking. Remember that, she adds. As she explains to me how the world has stopped looking back at her—as if the changes are all out there and not in her at all, I can almost believe she isn't leaving us. This is my quiet time, she says, looking at me kindly, telling me, as she always has, the things she never says to Gordon. She can say them to me because she always assumes I won't understand. In a way, it *is* selfish of her. I know her life is filled with guilty pleasures, always has been. I want to believe she is very selfish. She is so curious about the physical world. Everything around her is endlessly fascinating to her. Her otherworldliness comes out of the intensity of her immersion. Why shouldn't she enjoy herself more than other people? I wish for her to have had all the pleasure in the world. I hope she did.

Edith will be last among her sisters to die. It pains her to be going ahead of Gordon, although she takes some pleasure in that, too, in leaving him to tidy up and continue on after her. She'll never have to be alone here like he will.

Gordon tells me the story of how he and Edith met right after David and I get engaged, in 1991. I already know some of it because mama told me. But I haven't ever gotten the story from the horse's mouth. He wants to encourage us, to show David and me how to bring soulfulness and inventiveness to the pallid institution of marriage. The things you carry in your heart versus the law of the state. They may on the rare occasion be one and the same, but even then they are not the same.

Tuberculosis today is still a scourge, but not anything like what it was when Gordon and Edith suffered from it, when so many died. Their inseparability grew of out of this. As if they had met inside a rotting corpse and from this came their love and their discovery of how to live. Most of all, how their doctors, by forbidding them from having children, gave them the idea, and more than the idea, the motivation to do it. That's not just taking a chance. It is honing the sharp blade of living in the flames of death and persecution. You rise above the treeline, going from peak to peak, from scenic vista to scenic vista, death from tuberculosis the first and tallest. You come off it exhilarated. The next peak is death in childbirth, but you don't stop. It would have whisked her away at the very beginning of their life together. But not just her. I know Gordon. It would have taken him too. And you don't flinch, you're in it now. That's how I picture them, in my own way, listening to Gordon now. Miracle upon miracle of ordinary things. Just how they are. It occurs to me that I've never heard either one of them so much as raise their voice.

His face fills with joy as he tells me—because the surprise happy ending is just around the corner. Having been forbidden from having children. And then, their two strapping grown sons, Warren, now a celebrated newspaperman in New Zealand, Peter, a sculptor and builder of straw bale homes in Tucson. My friend wants me to see what can happen so long as we remain open to the possibility of miracles even in the shadow of death.

First thing the next morning, Gordon calls me on the phone he almost never uses to tell me Edith has left us. I run over to see him. I sit alone in the front room until the ambulance comes, while Gordon sits with Edith in their bedroom, she on their bed and he in the chair next to it. They come in, and bring her out on a gurney, her face covered. Gordon accompanies them as far as the road, and then comes back to sit with me for awhile.

It occurs to me for the first time on the day she dies that Edith has been in a physical contest every single day to do the things she does. There are no stairs in their home. She doesn't carry things. She lets Gordon do all the lifting and carrying. But I see now it's because she can't do these things. She doesn't have the strength. The hated young doctors, those arrogant men down in Saranac Lake, they weren't wrong. They just didn't understand the force in her that offset her physical weakness.

I've met Peter, and Warren. Both are big barrelchested men like lumberjacks. At the age I am I have to look almost straight up to look eye to eye with them.

I think of her with her paint box, going off into the day, me following her. Those walks too are acts of will. She chooses to do them *because* they are almost impossibly strenuous activities for her

Now that Edith has died, I suddenly understand that she was always choosing necessity and refusing necessity. With one lung, watercolors were a little more manageable than painting in oils would have been. They chose her. She'd be spending her life sitting so why not be sitting down and painting? Her sons are miracles of love and fortitude and the detritus of recklessness and willfulness. When I meet the burley boys, now grown men, there is something in their eyes that is opaque to me, though they both have it. Now that Edith has died, I think I know what that look was: It was nothing less than gratitude that *they* had not killed her, that they did not have to have that on their consciences.

The way Gordon tells it, Edith risks her life when she defies her doctors—who've just rescued her. Gordon would have said, It's up to you, my dear. And Edith would have answered, Oh, let's try. It would have felt right to them both. It captures that quality they share, the stubbornness. They would feel glad to count their own lives as of small account before their greater fascination with the wondrous things they can do now that they've found each other and are willing to take some chances.

One of them probably says, We are being foolish you know, and the other saying, Yes, very likely.

Imagine wanting something very badly, and getting it, the thing you want. Then you risk it all, everything. You cast aside the happiness you have found for something you don't particularly wish for, something you haven't thought much about. And imagine doing that being just the thing. Imagine that.

I ask Gordon now, Where do you think romantic love fits in life?

Gordon answers, It *is* life, the whole thing.

It's late spring of a new year, 1985. I'm thirteen. I like to walk into Ashland on my own in the morning sometimes, usually on Saturdays, to sit in the little park in the center of town with a Seven Up in the dappled sunlight and the breeze if there is one. It's a city park in a country town, at the intersection of all the main streets and thoroughfares, and with a glimpse of the river before it disappears under the bridge.

One of those Saturdays I meet a young woman there, watching her two small children. We start talking, sitting on the same bench, her kids playing all over the park, the water flowing by a stone's throw away at the bottom of the little hill we're on. She has a lot to say, speaking to me like we're old friends, her eyes on her kids, telling me her story. Her name is Martha.

Martha's from Maine, on the run from her younger child's father, who put his hands on her. I know this is something that happens. I've seen it in men's eyes and in women's eyes. But it is something that's never said. You might have words to say someone drinks, or is sick. But the beatings that happen behind closed doors in people's homes, no, no one talks about it.

I guess because the thing that would be talked about it is when it doesn't happen, the few cases. And maybe the only reason Martha can say the things she's saying is because she's not from here.

I like Martha very much. She is bold in a very matter of fact way, not bragging, just not silenced. Even though I am only thirteen, I feel between us a womanly bond, a bond of the marrow. She's named her older boy Justice, and the younger girl, just two years old, Liberty. She is not afraid of words. No, she knows their power!

Martha is short and sturdily built, but other than that an astonishing beauty, shapely, with stirring almond eyes. She's been renting a place here in Ashland for awhile, maybe a month or two, while she still has some money left. She tells me, Ashland is a bad town, and I should never trust any Ashland men, since the good ones leave as soon as they have the chance, and the ones who stay just want to prey on the women. She says she and her children have been picked up and abandoned by two men already in Ashland, and that now she's just looking for a way to leave. She says no one wants to help her here. And, as I listen, the very idea of a person's life ever getting this bad is brought home to me now for the very first time.

I've never met or heard about people as uncaring as she is describing. The funny thing is, the rawness of her interpretation of the world she lives in impresses me. She says, Love and lovelessness sleep side by side. Says it twice in the hour we're talking. She's named her children, signposted them, with humankind's two best ideas, declared herself a believer in Liberty and Justice—after making her own versions. She knows how to navigate the tricky currents, it seems to me, of the circumstances of her life. I listen, I believe her, and I believe in her. A strange picture passes through my brain of the men of Ashland drawing bitterness out of the land and brutalising women. And I can't help feeling a searing moment of pride knowing that my father was one of the good ones who left. This afternoon in the spring of my thirteenth year is the first time I think seriously of leaving.

Everything Martha tells me is two things—a show of the strength in her even as it is a confession of her weakness. I don't have to take her word for anything. I'm sure I know good men in this town. What's an Ashland man anyway? There's no such thing. Every one has their own story that's different from every other one's. Most aren't from here originally. Their people came from somewhere else anyway. The kind of Ashland men Martha is referring to are here too. I see them, with hollow eyes, the kind of men that will take advantage of a young woman who comes here with her two kids to get free of somebody. But that's not all there is here.

Fully five years after I meet Martha, in the heat of another summer, I set out one early afternoon to walk to town. It's a Saturday in July or August of 1990. I'm eighteen. Almost as soon as I turn on to the road, a car stops, and I get a ride the rest of the way. I look over at the man driving and we start talking. There's something about him. I'm curious because he seems to be from here and at the same time not to be like anybody I know. He is driving with his right hand while his left does a little dance on the steering wheel. He seems awfully glad to see me, though we haven't met before that I know of. A moment before, it was just me and whatever was on my mind, mama and my impending departure to live on my own in Plymouth mostly. And now sitting in this man's car I find I'm very interested in this person. It isn't what he's saying exactly. It's that he waits a beat before speaking. And the way he's listening to the things I'm saying makes me think he finds me refreshing. I don't think he knows what he's going to say until he hears himself say it. I get that impression. I like that about him too.

I am reasonably shy and wouldn't usually start talking to a strange man in a car, but for some reason I am panicking with excitement—in a good way. It isn't as if I'd taken one of mama's pills. I'm not high. But I am almost eighteen and a half. I say to him, Hey, I think I know you from somewhere.

He looks at me, really looks, like he's counting the freckles on my face, and says, No, I don't think so.

If you want to talk more, we can pull over before we get into town, I say. And now I am suddenly feeling scared, not of him, but of my own self. I look out at the roadside scenery and there are tears rolling down my cheeks because I'm laughing and at the same time I'm not in control. I'm upset with myself when I reach over to touch him because it is like I am reaching over to touch some part of my own innermost spot. If I can do this, I mean, seriously, what can't I do? I'm laughing hard again at my own outspokenness. What I want to do right now is also the thing I would want least to do in the world. But I'm staying in touch with my most sensitive spot. It is my way through from no place to some place. I am so delighted. I can't even describe how revved up and happy I feel. My little finger connects back to the rest of me, reaches the whole way back through to the very depth of me, like a fast-forward fantasy in reverse—a re-winding reality coming at me from some future me. That finger, the one I touch him with, is hard, it's true and it's mine.

There's a double turning where the road takes a steep curve downward, hiccoughing right and then flipping left on to a long straightaway vista. There are a few trailer homes here that over time have grown into pretty nice places, with cared-for lawns and plantings around them. There's a black and white MIA flag outside one, on a white flag pole with an American flag above it. And then we are beside the long field that has always meant something special to me for being wide open and at the same time contained by the straight lines of its rectangular shape.

He pulls over, and we both seem to become aware at the

same time that we haven't said our names. I tell him mine. He comedically offers his hand and says a name I've never heard before, which is Stanton. Beside the wide-open field in the box lines of its boundaries, we are wide-open and boxed in too. Orderly things, even just orderly-looking things, always enter strangely into the disorder of my world. On the hills beyond the rectangular field there are still some apple trees bearing fruit now. The short, fat, craggy trees rise and fall across the rising and falling hillocks like a procession of good souls. There's a low stone wall beyond them that's only more or less plumb, as if drawn by an aged master draftsman with a shaky hand. I say to Stanton, Don't you think it's all so beautiful?

After a pause he says, You'll see the departure of the orchards in maybe five or six years. You'd have thought it would take centuries. But it'll happen all of a sudden.

You don't know that, I say, incredulously. I'm taken aback by something I hear now for the first time in his voice, some misery or unkindness in him.

I do, he says. I've seen it happen already in other places. All that will be left of the apple orchards' unending rows will be two or three trees congregating under the lip of an exposed hillside, or in the groove of a stream bed at the bottom of a field, where they're spared the worst weather.

Then he smiles and raises both hands like he were sleepwalking and says, Only if I close my eyes will I see, impossibly, one spread its wings on high ground, its branches raised over a rounded hilltop, a bit bigger than all the others swarming below it, this one spreading tree lending the scene an intolerable rightness I will find nowhere else. Smiling myself, I close my eyes and picture it. Then I open my eyes and he reaches out his arm to me.

I think my boldness startles Stanton at first, and then finds its echo in the boldness in him, which must be why he kisses me now, which is exactly what I was hoping he'd do.

Then he sits back again, he's talking, and there is in his voice this warmth that is growing. It didn't start out as anything that strong, but it is becoming something and since he himself seems wary of it, I'm wary too.

Stanton tells me about his wife, who died, not very recently but not so long ago either. His true beloved he says. And her illness didn't take that away, so neither did her dying, he adds. But here he finds himself all alone just the same. And he looks at me with the most curious expression. It doesn't express sadness. More like the fight he's putting up *against* the enveloping expanse of sadness. Whatever it is, I don't have words for, maybe love or hope, I don't know. He even smiles again, as if to say, These are the colors and the shapes. Or even, These are some colors and some shapes. He's almost eighteen and a half, just like me. And I'm whatever age he is—forty? Fifty?—just the same as him.

I kiss him again, and hold him tightly, then sit back and laugh, and we laugh together a little too. No hurry to go anywhere in particular now.

So long as we aren't alone, anything is bearable. And when we're alone nothing is really bearable, so we just have to pretend, and keep going.

Stanton says, as if just mentioning something that isn't necessarily so important but he's saying it anyway, that burying his wife wasn't hard, but going on afterward without her was.

No kids? I ask. He shakes his head.

Is it such a mystery I'm captivated by this man? Making his way determinedly while grief-stricken, or so it seems to me. How shaken he is, drifting, unmoored, the brokenness of him unbroken.

Stanton is a good-looking man, troubled looking, with a face that has character and modesty in it. If there's a problem it's that he knows he's attractive. I'm wishing that from time to time he would just step out of himself and touch me again, in the straightforward laughing way he was doing it. He knows he can. We've broken the ice already. It's no more dangerous now than if we were driving and stopped at one of those scenic vistas, where you look out and you breathe in and die just a little and then get back in the car and continue on your way. And he does, kisses me gently, just a touching of lips and then sits back and reaches out and holds my hand and he's crying now of course, with nothing more to say, and I let him and I'm with him. It's okay, I say, and it really is.

He says, People can get used to almost anything. Can and do.

He stops, sighs, is through with talking. I can see he's ready now. He wants to kiss me again. I want to too. I'm not unaffected by this man, by who he is and what he is. We're connecting and he's performing for me in everything he's saying, performing just for me. He moves me. Despite our differences, in age and everything else, we're the same. I mourn in the same way he does, and there's happiness in him that's just like mine.

I push him off me and I say, not unkindly, I have to go. I'm scared, but although I don't say so, I'm also ready. Scared and curious. Wet and needy. Scared not so much of him. I know he will stop if I ask him to. Mostly of myself, of the power in me which is without end. I go from feeling love for this stranger to feeling an even greater love for myself. It washes over me and is the strangest thing ever. The power to give yourself to someone, to give yourself lightly and easily. And the power to take yourself back.

There is the weight of him, how good it is to feel it. How ready I am to hold somebody, to be underneath him, a man not a boy. But then I get in my own way, that's what's happening. Who is this person?! I'm asking, not about him but about me. As willing as I am to be under him, to inhale the good taste of his breath, to look into the desire in his eyes that is like the awakening of a slumbering beast, I feel huge relief as I get free of him. My heart is racing, and my heart is my own. It is ahead of me. I can only see a little way in what feels to me like a black darkness. I can follow it now, my racing heart, I have to. I can let it lead me to him, or away from him. The hard part is to let it lead me back to myself, always back to myself, whether it is someplace I inhabit alone or not alone. It is the one imperative. For me to be with me.

I become lost to myself, all the more so the harder I look. It is a terrible moment, the very worst. To be not alone and to have lost myself, to be crowded into an unwelcome aloneness beside another person. It is like not being able to breathe, a suffocating moment that goes on. Time stops, not in a good way.

Maybe something similar is happening to Stanton. Our happiness together and then each of us alone in our misery. He doesn't move as I reach my arm behind me finally, open the car door and begin to ease my body out, watching him all the while. If he had pulled away from me this way, suddenly, like I am doing, I would have held on to him and stopped him from going. But since it is me separating myself from him, of course he just lets me. Now that I'm free to go, I stop myself. I want him to keep me here in the absolute stillness of the stopped car. I'd hold on to me if I were him. I'm feeling clairvoyant today. We are the same. What hurts him is in me too, and this thing we have in common is what led me to be so free with him in the first place and also what scares me. For lack of a better word, I can call it our otherworldliness. What is this world to us when we inhabit another world of our own making?

There is a word I learn from a teacher at school who used to be a nun, or at least was training to become one before she leaves her order to become a teacher and somehow ends up in Ashland. The word is *misericordia*. It means pity. She's a pretty, no, she is a beautiful woman, soulful looking, *transcendant* looking, one of those people that seem to have come out of the sky, a tourist here on earth who finds our ways and traditions quaint and entertaining set against the terrifying and maddening realities of her order of angels in the skies above, where there is no such thing exactly as death or human suffering, but where nonetheless there is pain and joy, brevity in eternity, feuds and wars, alongside happiness unending.

The teacher's name is Eleanor. When we learn Latin phrases from her, she has an expression on her lips of profound mischief, almost like she were taking the most sacred things she knows and turning them into a practical joke she is playing on us, all in good fun. *Domine non sum dignus*, which curiously some of the kids know already from Catholic services, but they were never told what it means. How *Lord, I am not worthy* expresses our readiness and worth, borne in humility and even despair. It means the opposite of what it says, in other words. And my Eleanor days are school days I am thankful for, because I wouldn't want to receive this news from anyone but her.

You would think that someone as beautiful as Eleanor would have large, almond-shaped eyes, blue-green maybe, or any color, but piercing. Instead hers are these little red rabbit's eyes, and her loveliness resides in her whole being with eyes that struggle to keep up with the rest of her. I hardly know her, and yet I do know her. She is one of my people, who abandon the way that has been laid out for them, not because it's bad but because they are uncontainable. About *misericordia*, what she says is, It is what we feel for the poor of spirit.

As I look back at the car, I can only see that Stanton is still sitting more or less as I left him. I cannot read his facial expression or what his body is saying at this moment either. There's steam drifting off the hood, but he doesn't drive off. I decide that I could love this man or someone like him when I'm ready, someone who's eccentric and has the classical features of an old car with dents and some rust on it and speaks the way Stanton does. I thank God Stanton has no idea what I'm thinking. And then I leave him there and move on to follow the road into town. As I walk along there comes over me indescribable apprehension. There is so much for me here. There is nothing here for me. I'll never make a life for myself here.

Some birds are completely nondescript until they take wing, when you see a streak of red or yellow under the wing that was hidden before. You might think the effect would be funny, but it isn't, it's breathtaking—a moving arrow of color, noble, dramatic, intelligent. A harmonious picture. A vanishing line in the air drawn with tremendous quickness.

I have a fantasy of myself standing beside my father on mama's porch, or sitting there together with him, just watching birds fly over the field, not doing anything else, just him and me standing next to each other, not touching.

When I close my eyes, I can almost feel a hard place begin to form inside me, like a good and familiar object, a pen or a ball, or like holding someone's hand that holds yours in return.

I had started out that afternoon with the sun firmly overhead, and as I passed under trees on the way to the main road, it darted around me. Now the sun is a white fluorescence high over the western mountains, and the shadows it makes are long and narrow. They tremble in the wind as I walk through them. To the north gray clouds are massing, and I can see by the thick haze over the hills the places where it's raining. That weather's moving this way, but I can't tell yet how quickly or whether it might change again before it gets here. Having come this far, I want to walk the short rest of the way into town. Somewhere behind me the man I met still sits in his car, or has driven off. Stanton and I didn't exchange our numbers. I didn't think about it. Maybe he didn't either. What will be will be. Sitting on the stone steps in front of the Five and Dollar, I can't stop my mind from wanting to know where he is. Part of me wants to go looking for him. I'm a kaleidoscope. And suddenly all I want is a friend my own age. I want Marie. I don't hate Stanton or anybody, only my loneliness.

As I walk home the sweeping gray and white sky is darkening like a descending curtain. The frost heaves in the road are like slow-motion convulsions. The abandoned railroad tracks that run beside the road are eerily alive like the trains were running every hour in some parallel universe. I find this comforting in the same way hummingbirds are, or even chipmunks and squirrels or snakes, signs of completely different life forms. A Schwann's Frozen Foods truck passes. I turn the last corner onto our sandy road that dips once to the old stone bridge and then rises gradually up, like a short in-breath and a longer out-breath. Arriving home, I see mama has put out the big tin wash-basin to catch rainwater. This time of year we always worry the spring might go dry. The car isn't here. She's gone for one of her drives. I reach our covered porch as the first drops land in a harsh, percussive eruption of sound that passes through me from the soft ends of my fingers and toes to the tips of my ears. All across the stamped circular corrugations of the tub the rain plucks knots of sound that ring out. And then it's coming down heavily, furiously, in sheets. I sit on the porch in my favorite chair, the white wicker one with flowering cushions and room to spare. Rain is ricocheting onto my feet and it's a little damp all over already. I pull my feet up under me. The tub off in the distance is gradually filling and as the water rises the muffled sound grows quieter. The droplets fall in a soft drum roll now. I am here. I am part of this. Who could ask for anything more? The rocking chair rocks me lopsidedly, the house behind me swaying from side to side. The rain falling on the fields rises back up as mist in a glow almost like moonlight. The smell of plant life and dirt in the air is like the smell of bread baking. The lines between things shimmer. There is, everywhere, the feeling of spirit pulling matter along, the way a child can pull an adult, the lighter vessel prevailing over the heavier one, a kind of happiness in that.

Since I belong only to myself, I cannot be taken. But oh how I wish I could! Why must I be like a stick stuck in a rushing torrent? I want to float away, to feel under me the pulse of the rushing water. I'd like to be subsumed, and reliant, to please someone, some man, to withstand and to love him. Am I not too adamant, too much my own lost soul to ever find real comfort in someone else? It hurts so much just simply to be me. Why is that? Does it have to be so?

I never do see Stanton again, or Martha for that matter. The kind of angels they were, who could help me when they could not help themselves, maybe I'll never meet that kind again.

I think of Gordon. More than anything else, I just want to watch the world go by and not be alone, just like him. And I think of Martha, though I only met her that once. On the move. With two children, and no money, no hesitation. Just how amazing she is! Her children are her inspiration and motivation, the engine powering her up, but her strength comes from within. I haven't experienced her as desperate at all. When she says love and lovelessness sleep side by side, to me it's as if she's saying, I have everything I need in me.

And then mama is back, with a light ignited in her eyes! And I can laugh out loud to see that the hours away from me were just the best thing for her, the break she needed more than anything.

My whole life I've been looking for a place to write, a room or whatever. And I haven't found it yet. The heaviest thing I own is my portable typewriter. It is like a stack of bricks, a stack of bricks in a hard black plastic case with a handle that I carry everywhere I go like a crazy person. The things I write about, the places and the people, aren't ever portable though. As much as I wish they would be, they don't come unstuck, my words notwithstanding. Not to make a joke of it, but it is as if the hundreds of pages I have written in Geoff's class about everything and everyone under the sun were all nothing more than portraits of my heavy little portable typewriter itself, nothing more.

My father, now that I know him a little, told me that the hardest thing he ever did was to leave mama and me and all the rest that Ashland was to him. He also said he was never able to finish leaving. The break he made physically was never complete. And for all the time that has passed since that day, when I was four and he was nineteen and my mama was only twenty-one, only a little more than a year older than I am now, a part of him has been waiting as if it was no time at all. The way he says these things, I know they're true.

No one made you go, I say.

No, he agrees. I chose.

It was Gordon that put the idea into my head of going to see him. Maybe now would be the right time to do it, he said—not because it will change anything for you. It won't. And maybe that's why. This was back when David and I were about to be married, and I think that was true then. I'm not sure about now.

Does he remember that Willow Lake turns slightly on its axis, like a crooked finger? Perhaps he doesn't think about it, however many times he once entered the body of this lake and went out onto it, the same as me. Does he know that even the hardest ice is a liquid slowly moving? I'll never be able really to talk to him until we have spoken about this.

We never claim to own the water and we don't ever feel like we own the land either, though my father's mother has deeded it to us now. Our boundaries here are the deaths of people and whatever else happens, all the comings and goings. There is solace and at the same time we are more exposed than we would be anywhere else. In this paradise that Edith calls habitable, you can be happy but you don't ever forget. If we had hoped to be spared here, what happens instead is nearly the very opposite. We have fewer defenses than we might have in some other place.

The attraction of cities has to be, it seems to me, that they constantly pave over, rebuild, cover up, forget and replace the past. Will my father one day teach me all about that? I wonder, with only the wind in the trees now to answer me. Maybe his having moved away helps me, in the same way that my grandmother's departure in some ways does. They are explorers we have sent out to discover the world for us. He went so that one day I might follow. But did he think that neither his presence nor his absence mattered? That mama and I too would be whatever we would be, with or without him? No, if he understood that much he probably would have stayed, for that would have meant he felt a part of our geographies, the inner and the outer ones, and accepted his place in our lives and then why leave? There had to be other reasons. And he must have understood that he was abandoning us. Were I not a daughter without a father, would I know myself differently than I do, better than I do? So many questions, never a last question. I am becoming less and less interested in them. Body of water, daughter of this place, let me make something of this body of water that I am.

His hands are shaking. Just a little, but there's no mistaking it. It can only mean he's a little afraid of me. If my own father is afraid of me then all is lost. I don't want him to be afraid, not even a little.

He tells me he thinks of me often, counting out how old I am now each time from one year to the next. He says remembering I'm out there somewhere in the world growing up, finding my way, always raises his spirits. I think of the Sam Cooke song, *I love you . . . for sentimental reasons.* But you don't say it if it isn't true.

He says: I left Ashland literally without thinking what I was doing. But from the minute I got here a few days later I always knew there would come a day when you and I would be sitting here talking just like we are. I've known all this time that there would be things I would never understand until you and I try to understand them together.

His words are falling into me and I am scrutinizing them. It is too soon and too late. Too soon to say them, and too late for an apology. All I know already is that this will never be about understanding. He moved on, and so will I. There's no understanding any of it.

I keep saying to myself: He doesn't know I'm pregnant. He just thinks I'm a little fat. He looks to me like a well tended potted plant, one that gets all the sun it needs and the right amount of water. But make no mistake, by seeking him out I've opened a window into a hurricane. Cars and houses are flying through the air.

It is late June, 1989, the fifth anniversary of Jennie leaving us. Mama and I are spending the day here together quietly. The rain arrives in the afternoon. At first it is the sound of a thousand heartbeats, tapping everywhere. We come outside to sit on the porch and listen. The sky lays over us like an oil cloth. Even before the rain begins, the sun is only a slight tightening across the morning sky. And now, through the sounds of the waves of water softly drumming on our shingled roof and tap-tapping on the tin roof of the barn, the barrage of thunder and lightning shakes us and terrifies old Julius. One sudden, short report—a sharp splitting sound that follows a lightning flash and thunder clap, very close—is the decapitation of the tallest pine at the top of the driveway, the one nearest to the house. We see the top branches come apart and fall through the lower stories of itself, the smell of burning wood in the air. The lightning comes and goes so fast there isn't time for the tree to die. It will live on.

The next day is gentle and still in the wake of yesterday's disturbance. We walk among the fallen and broken bits, inhaling the aroma of soft wood and mashed ferns, fragrant like nothing else. In the woods whole colonies of new mushrooms in improbable shapes and colors are already erupting, clinging to the bark and dead branches of other felled trees. More trees fall for days, out of view yet near enough that we hear them, the sound like bone snapping. And tiny wild orchids are suddenly everywhere among the tall grasses, with purple dots and yellow-spotted sacs tilting on their spindly stems. As our eyes grow accustomed, we notice other miniature wild flowers, an explosion of them—orange balls, black-eyed Susans, delicate, populous jewels in white and yellow and purple, turning our fields out, although still mostly invisible until you start to really look for them.

Let me not be one of them, one of the many who belong nowhere. Let me have this place of my own making.

I turn twenty like a coiled spring. Perfection is getting pregnant right after David and I decide to end things.

~

Our sixteen acres are populous with blueberries, blackberries, raspberries, and strawberries, smaller than the cultivated kinds, with a slightly bitter aftertaste, and roughness that scratches the roof of your mouth like someone had stirred dirt and sand into their sweetness. The strawberry vines, low to the ground in the fields, bloody the tops of our bare feet. The blueberries are thrown across the tops of the bushes in constellations, imprinting the day as the stars above do the clear black nights. And sometimes they're also sewn into the underbrush in pockets hidden from the eye but where your hands find them by their smoothness. The raspberry buttons lean towards us on high stalks from flower beds where no one intended them to be, and from the edges of the fields their soft caps spill into our hands one by one. The blackberries cluster on a hillside in the woods, and when we follow the path to reach them it's always with a tingle down our spine because bear also gather there to eat them.

Mama supplements our berries with cultivated ones she buys at Longwood Farms. She slow-cooks the jam on the stove in soup pots, then spoons it into mason jars to set. We melt the wax in a little pan, then pour it over the jam. Breaking the wax seals will be one of the ritual acts of winter, our triumph lying in how our jam supply outlasts the freeze most winters.

Mama's jam is good and nutty. This year we're making jam as we always have. But it's just pretending we're still the same when we aren't.

~

Coming back from mama's house a few weeks after my twentieth birthday, I have my accident. I'm not eating. I have so much on my mind. When mama gets up to make herself something, I go outside and smoke four cigarettes. I don't have any Valiums left and for some reason I'm not feeling kind enough towards myself to want to go and seek relief. I want to tough things out.

What I remember isn't the crash. It is, just before, either awakening or falling asleep to the comforting growl of the car's engine, and noting the time, around 5:00 in the afternoon. An orchestra is playing on the radio.

I haven't passed Crystal Springs yet, but that's just ahead, and with all my windows open I'm inhaling the primordial coolness of the place, the rhythm and flow it has—though I'm not stopping, so it normally passes in the blink of an eye. Before cracking all those ribs and my collarbone, before I create the scar that I will later call my boundary line, I remember wanting to stay and let everything go on without me, signing off the faster moving slow-moving track to get on the slower moving one, knowing this will hurt but not wanting to think about that.

Lying in the cot in hospital, I decide I'll move back with mama for a while. But when I get out I return to my apartment. When David arrives, I tell him that he has to leave at the end of the school year, and I'll stay with mama meanwhile, but then I'm coming back. I want him gone. I'm happy to be pregnant, but you couldn't imagine a less happy version of the happy pregnant me than this one. And when mama helps me move back at the beginning of June, the emptiness there is almost more than I can take.

One day, still wearing my arm in a sling and the collar around my neck from the accident, it occurs to me that I've stopped writing. I've been for an afternoon walk. I'm returning over the shiny new steel bridge into Plymouth on my way to work, feeling detached in the way you do when you know that the only thing the hours ahead mean to you is $5.65 an hour. I am smoking. And it suddenly occurs to me that I haven't written anything new in nearly three months, like when you suddenly realize you haven't eaten all day, the thought coming before any pangs of actual hunger, like it has nothing to do with you yet.

My view north from halfway across is of the Pemigewasset River shorn and white and sandy, broad and turbulent and very light-filled. It reminds me of a tin cup being shaken, heaped with silver and copper coins, the light falling differently on the hand than on the cup, bleaching the battered cup, yellowing the hand. And since this view of the river flowing down into Plymouth, or more exactly, next to Plymouth, from the north country is a favorite of mine at any time of year, I'd normally have taken out my journal and a pencil and stood there writing for a few minutes, writing down how I see it on this particular day. But that isn't who I am right now. I haven't really thought about how I might be changing, or not changing. In class I've been plucking over-ripe fruit, fragments from an earlier time, waiting to see if Geoff will have the dog sense to notice. He doesn't. I haven't recognized the effect not writing is having on me. I keep on walking to arrive at the store on time, thinking as I walk how I've stopped writing and didn't notice and how amazing is that? I realize I'm going to have to face up to myself sometime soon now. I'm smoking, but I'm pregnant now too, which means one of us is going to have to get out of town, like in a Western. Now I understand what the smoking is about. It's to protect me from the pregnant girl. Marie must have known this. It's why she hasn't told me to stop. Oh, God.

You've all but completed a book, you know, in the pieces you've written for me, Geoff says. What will you call it?

Ashland, I say.

But there's no book, I add.

I see, Geoff says.

This morning I dreamt of his city and of an ocean liner that passes by on its way up the Hudson River in the gray light of pre-dawn, all dolled up in yellow and green and blue and red lights strung across its bow and its upper decks. In the dream I am at my father's again, looking out, watching the august lumbering glacier of a vessel moving upriver with an indescribable heavy grace. I see the giant silent ship and I feel its power.

In the early morning dark, when I cannot sleep, I place my hands on my belly and I make lists in my mind of the people I know, the dead and the living. Thinking of them one after another, I attach words like clothing to their nakedness. I do this over and over.

About the Author

Dan Simon is the founder and editor-in-chief of Seven Stories Press. *Ashland* is his debut novel. He lives in New York and New Hampshire.